D1482807

AIRFIELD

AIRFIELD

Jeanette Ingold

HARCOURT BRACE & COMPANY

San Diego   New York   London

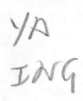

Requests for permission to make copies of any part of the work
should be mailed to:
Permissions Department, Harcourt Brace & Company,
6277 Sea Harbor Drive, Orlando, Florida 32887-6777.

Library of Congress Cataloging-in-Publication Data
Ingold, Jeanette.
Airfield/by Jeanette Ingold.
p.   cm.
Summary: In 1933, fifteen-year-old Beatty hangs around a small
Texas airport waiting for visits from her pilot-father from whom
she longs to learn about her deceased mother.
[1. Fathers and daughters—Fiction.   2. Sex roles—Fiction.
3. Airports—Fiction.   4. Airplanes—Fiction.]   I. Title.
PZ7.I533Ai   1999
[Fic]—dc21   99-6086
ISBN 0-15-202053-5

Text set in Ehrhardt
Designed by Ivan Holmes
First edition
F E D C B A
Printed in the United States of America

This is a work of fiction. All names, characters, and
organizations, all places and events are fictional. Any
resemblance to any organization or to any actual person,
living or dead, is unintended.

For my parents, Jim and Carey Reilly

Acknowledgments

The Muddy Springs Airport and the airline it serves are fictional, but the idea for this book came from stories my parents told of the days when my dad first worked for American Airlines—American Airways, then—in a job very similar to Grif Langston's. Dad was part of the airline for forty years, but his best tales came from that time when commercial aviation was a brash adolescent trying hard to grow up.

I'm indebted to many people for helping pin down the details of what flying was like in the early 1930s: Ben Kristy, curator of the American Airlines C. R. Smith Museum in Fort Worth, and the museum's director, Jay Miller; Colonel Knox Bishop (USAF/Ret.), curator of the Frontiers of Flight Museum in Dallas; and, at the University of Texas at Dallas, Dr. Larry D. Sall, associate library director for special collections, and the History of Aviation Collection volunteers who let me listen in on their hangar flying.

I'm grateful, too, for assistance from fliers and aviation experts Otto Becker, Jack Callaway, Gregory Kennedy, Nancy Robinson Masters, Mary and John Stevenson, and John Talbot, and for the helpful staffs and wonderful resources of the Texas State Library and the Center for American History at the University of Texas at Austin.

1

*A*IRFIELD?" THE OLD GUY sorting radiator caps in front of Joe's Texas Auto Parts sends a dented cap spinning to a junk heap. "You goin' flyin', young lady?"

"I wish I were! But I'm just taking a late lunch to my uncle. He's filling in for the station manager."

"I guessed you was new here. That turn's another mile on."

"Oh…" I rub the back of my neck, lifting away hair wet with perspiration. Dark patches of sweat pock the front of my dress. "I'd hoped I was closer."

Out on the otherwise empty highway, a worn automobile struggles our way. Its outside bristles with tied-on house goods, and the inside is packed with people. Depression migrants, I suppose, like half the world seems to be this June of 1933.

"I reckon," Joe says, "you could take that old farm track past my billboard. It'd be a bit of a shortcut."

There's the sudden *craack* of a tire blowing out, and the car we've been watching lurches to a lopsided halt.

The first out is a boy who looks to be a couple of years older than me, perhaps nearer seventeen than my almost-fifteen. *Dirt poor*...It's a fleeting thought, gone as fast as I can feel bad for thinking it.

But, truthfully, he does look about as ragtag as the vehicle itself.

"They ain't gonna have no money," Joe says, as though he's already hearing the whole conversation, him trying to sell a replacement and the family wanting whatever threadbare tire he'll give for free.

"Yeah. Well," I answer, feeling for him and them both, "I ought to be getting along. Will that shortcut take me straight to the airport?"

"Close enough, anyway."

I'm soon thinking that Joe and I have different ideas about just what a shortcut is. Going the extra mile on the highway would have been quicker than this. Twice I have to pull my dust-coated bicycle under barbed wire strung across the old roadbed.

I keep remembering that migrant family, wondering if they left a place like this, land once farmed but now surrendered to mesquite and cactus. Or maybe they're from a place where pine trees close in, or where vines smother?

Or maybe they didn't ever have a place?

Of course, I remind myself, *I don't have a place, either.*

That is, I do, only it rotates, aunt to aunt. Yesterday it was with Aunt Fanny in Dallas and would have stayed so all summer if that storm hadn't blown a tree down through the roof of her house.

It was easy enough, though, to catch an early bus here, to Clo and Grif and their temporary home at the Muddy Springs Hi-Way Tourist Court. And if this doesn't work out, my barging in on what's still almost their honeymoon, I can always move on to Aunt Maud in Waco.

Though I'm hoping it does work out. Clo's more like a sister than an aunt, fifteen years closer to my age than Fanny and Maud are. She's always made me feel that having me is pleasure rather than duty, and I hope her being married won't change that.

It won't, I think, laughing again at how she met my bus this morning, bursting aboard, all red curls and wiry energy, to hug me before I could even get out of my seat.

Abruptly, the old roadbed comes to an end, and I see in the distance a hangar. Next to it, a smaller building with a huge MUDDY SPRINGS painted on its roof must be the terminal where Grif is working.

And between me and the buildings there's a long, hard-packed dirt clearing, which, after a moment, I realize is the landing field. Its only marking is a huge embedded circle, for identification, I suppose, though I bet from the air it looks more like a target. Instead of runways there are just sun-baked furrows showing all the ways planes have come in.

I'm bouncing my way across the field, thinking Joe and I also have different ideas about "close enough," when I hear the faint sound of a motor.

I stop to search the sky.... *There it is ...*

Shading my eyes, I watch a speck of rosy orange and yellow come closer and take the shape of a small, single-engine biplane. And then it dawns on me: The plane is getting ready to land on this field that I'm in the middle of.

I quickly get back on my bike, hop a few steps to get started, stand on the pedals to pick up speed.

The engine sound grows louder incredibly fast, and when I

look behind me the plane is at the back corner of the field, coming in on a low diagonal.

Briefly I wonder if the pilot can even see me, if maybe the dust all over my clothes might make me seem to be part of the field. I wave and my front wheel catches in a rut and throws me onto a stubble of dry weeds and gritty earth. There's not even time to get to my feet....

And then, just as the plane seems to be almost on top of me, it swoops up in a steep climb. The gold lines on its side flash by so fast they look like bolts of lightning, and I glimpse a pilot fighting to gain height.

In no more than an instant the aircraft has cleared the nearest corner of the field and is climbing away.

I brush off my dress, untangle a tumbleweed from my bike spokes, and try to calm down. I'll give Grif his lunch and then get away from the airport before that pilot circles around and comes looking for me.

But even as I'm wheeling my bicycle along, avoiding what looks like the most worn landing path, my eyes follow the airplane. A shiver races along my skin, a feeling hard to place. Still fear, maybe, but also thrill.

It's a feeling I get every time I watch a plane and imagine that I'm the one flying. What would it be like?

The airplane briefly disappears into a blinding dazzle of sunlight, and when I catch sight of it again it's shrunk to a glittering speck. Already it has soared so far, so fast, so *high*.

2

THERE'S NOBODY IN the main part of the small terminal building. Double doors on each end stand open to the breeze, and papers on a short counter flutter under the weight of a stapler and ticket punch. A chalkboard says the westbound flight is due in from Fort Worth at 1:59, to depart again sixteen minutes after that.

I can see it in the sky now, its deep-bellied body and single wing on each side as different from that other plane as can be. Still, the small one probably isn't far behind. Where's Grif?

Washing my face and hands quickly with water from a glass jug, I call, "Hello?"

A snatch of static leads me to the doorway of a tiny operations room where Grif sits at a table of radio equipment. He's wearing earphones and taking notes but waves a greeting when he notices my reflection in a mirror that hangs from a nail.

"Winds north at fifteen and gusting," I hear him repeat into a microphone. "Thanks, Sam."

Leaning forward so he sees, I put down his lunch and mouth the words "From Clo."

He nods, his eyes lighting up like she's done something a lot more wonderful than sending a ham sandwich that he forgot. He and my aunt have cared that way about each other since they were seniors in high school, half a dozen years ago, and I'm glad that he's finally got a job and they've been able to get married.

It's just a relief job. Grif has been hired by an airline to move about Texas filling in for station managers away on vacation or training. But it's work, and in aviation and using radios. To Grif, it must seem like incredible good fortune.

"I've got to go," I whisper, but he says, "Just give me a minute to relay this weather report." Flipping switches, he begins tapping teletypewriter keys. Then he adjusts more radio controls and identifies himself to the pilot of the westbound airliner. "You've got the skies to yourself," he says, "except for a small plane I heard fly over a bit ago—but it's apparently gone on. Come in whenever you're ready. And, Collin...she's here."

Collin!

As soon as Grif pulls off his earphones, even before I hug him hello, I ask, "Is Dad flying that plane?"

"He is. He traded routes with another pilot just to see you."

"And you and Clo wanted me to be surprised?"

Grif grins and nods, though he says, "Beatty, you realize your dad will be on the ground only long enough to refuel."

That's OK. Sixteen minutes is better than nothing. After yesterday's storm, things happened so fast Aunt Fanny and I never even learned if the telegram we sent Dad reached him, but I guess it must have.

I hope Grif's right about that pilot I want to avoid. Maybe he really has flown on somewhere else. I don't think he would have had a way to make a report about me. Until recently, even passenger planes didn't have two-way radios—I know that because I remember Dad talking about them being installed.

Still, Grif is looking closely at me now, taking in my scratches and the dirt on my dress. "What happened to you?" he asks.

"I fell off my bike—," I begin, but before I can decide how much to add, the telephone's ringing interrupts.

Grif picks up the receiver—"Yes, this is Muddy Springs"—and after a moment jots a note, which he hands to me.

"Beatty," he says, "will you run this over to the hangar while I bring your dad's plane in? Give it to Kenzie—he's the mechanic—and tell him it's about that part he's working on. El Paso needs it now."

"But—"

"It'll just take a minute."

The hangar's wide doors have been rolled back to open up the whole front. "Mr. Kenzie," I call, peering into a huge space where unlighted floodlights lamps hang from a grid of roof trusses. The building smells of the grease and motor oil soaked into the concrete floor. There're tools and equipment but no people.

A small truck rushes up behind me, MUDDY SPRINGS AIRPORT MOBILE SERVICE on its side. It brakes to a stop, and the driver jumps out.

"Mr. Kenzie?"

"Just Kenzie. I can't talk now." He hurries in a kind of limping run for several items that he throws in the back. "Catch me after I get that Ford Tri-Motor serviced."

"Tri–Motor…you mean the airplane? I think this note is about something that's supposed to go *on* it."

Kenzie reads the message and spits. "Somebody always wanting yesterday what I ain't ready to send. Come here."

He moves, his limp deeper now he's not running, to a work-bench where a piece of machinery soaks in a pan of kerosene. "Here," he says, sticking a brush in my hands, "clean that part and bring it out."

And then, just like that, he's gone, driving his service truck over to the plane that has now rolled to a stop near the terminal. I see Grif and him run a hose from the truck up onto a wing.

About a dozen thoughts tumble through my mind all at once, the main one being that I don't have time for this now.

And cleaning an airplane part! It's not a girl's job!

But I reach in and pick the piece up, surprised at how heavy it is. A splash of filthy liquid spreads an oily ring on my skirt.

Quickly I scrub the part and then hurry it out to the service truck. Kenzie scowls and tells me, "I said, 'Clean it *good*.'"

But Dad is running my way, swooping me up in a bear hug, standing me back so he can look at me. He searches my face like he's got to see for himself I'm not hurt, and I rush to explain that the scratches aren't anything, a bike fall.

"I'm fine, Dad. Truly. And Aunt Fanny is, too."

"Then you ride more carefully! And while you're at it, stay out of windstorms!"

That sets us both laughing, a relief that prompts Dad to tease, "Or did you wish up that storm yesterday just to throw off the Beatty Rotation?"

That's what the aunts call it, my annual calendar of living four months with each of them.

"And rotate myself to the middle of nowhere on purpose? You must be kidding!" Then I add, "But now that I'm here, maybe I'll get to see you a little more often? When you're here at the airport, I mean?"

"You know I rarely fly the transcontinental route," Dad answers, his attention already moved on. He's watching what's being done to his plane, glancing at his watch, observing the sky, and checking to see which way the wind sock is blowing.

It's how Dad always is, worried to make certain I'm safe and well but believing that's all that's important.

I can understand. He lost my mom, who died from pneumonia, when I was a year old. What I figure is that having someone he loved die was such an overwhelmingly *big* thing, it made him just shut down his feelings. And I guess it might explain why he won't talk about her.

Anyway, that was when the Beatty Rotation got started, when Dad first deposited me with his family and they began taking turns keeping me as they had time and could.

"Collin, is this that daughter you brag about?" The question comes from Dad's copilot. He's young and nice enough to grin at me and suggest, "So, does she get to do the next leg with us? There's extra seats."

The suggestion, coming so suddenly when for years I've been trying to talk Dad into taking me for a plane ride, about takes my breath away.

"Oh, Dad...Please? Can I?"

The copilot winks at me before adding, "My wife's in El Paso, Collin. She can put your daughter up for the night and see she gets on the flight back tomorrow morning."

Always before, Dad has had some reason to say no to me—

full loads, or I'm too young to manage the return trip by myself, or just, "Beatty, I don't want you flying, and that's that." But this time, maybe because the idea's come from someone else, Dad actually seems to be considering it.

Just then, though, a motor cuts the air, and the small biplane—the one I was wishing would just go away—lands and rushes toward us. As it slows to a stop the painted gold lightning on its side becomes just jagged stripes.

The pilot climbs down from the back of an open cockpit, pulling off a leather helmet and shaking out short, permed hair. *A woman!* She unsnaps the front of a leather flying suit as she strides toward us, showing a plain white shirt underneath. I hear her call to a staring passenger, "Yes, women can fly!"

And then she spots me. "You! I've got something to say to you."

She says it to everyone who's in earshot. "This *fool*…right in my landing path and about as visible as a scared jackrabbit… only good luck and a wind gust kept me from killing her."

She's still carrying on when she reaches us. "Any *child* should know not to wander about an airfield…Who's in charge here?"

"I am," Grif says, "but I don't understand. Did you try to land before?"

"Yes," she answers, "and I'd like to know why—"

"I'm sorry," I break in, embarrassed and wishing I'd told Grif right away about what happened. I don't want him blamed for something I did. "I was taking a shortcut, and nobody knew I was out there."

Grif, after a quick, disbelieving glance at me, repeats my apology.

But by now the pilot's gaze has settled on my father.

"Collin! Is that you? And…" She looks at me, and what seems like recognition sweeps her face. "Oh no, Collin. Is this your *daughter* I almost ran down?"

Then she gets really angry. "What are you doing, letting her grow up without good sense?"

Dad's face is rigid, his lips thin and tight. "Beatty," he says, "I want you to leave here now."

Chapter

3

I DON'T EVEN TRY the shortcut again but pedal furiously down Airfield Road and turn east onto the highway. *How could things have gone so wrong so fast?*

Nobody even let me explain. Or let me ask any questions.

Who is that woman? What business is it of hers how I'm raised? And how did she know who I am, anyway?

I don't even have a name for her, except to think of her as Gold Lightning. Her and her airplane both.

Dad was so angry he could hardly talk—far more than I deserved.

"Dad," I told him, "I did something stupid, but I didn't get hurt. Nobody did."

But he turned his back to me, rigid, with that tight control he shows when my mother is mentioned—and he never explains that, either.

"What are you so mad at?" I insisted.

But by then he was walking to his airplane, calling to the passengers, "Let's board."

———

Before I know it, I'm almost to Joe's Texas Auto Parts, and the scene there jerks my thoughts back to the present.

The old car is still in front, engine running and blown-out tire replaced, but the car's people are standing outside, arguing, it looks like.

A man flings himself away from them. He grabs together a small bundle of things and commences walking up the road toward me. Bitter voiced, he's talking to himself as we pass: "... won't go on, that's their doing. But I ain't goin' back."

The others, all except the boy I noticed before, get in the car. I reach them as a woman asks, "Moss, you comin' with us or goin' with your pa?"

The boy, looking as if neither's much of a choice, answers, "I guess I'll try here a spell, Ma."

His mother flinches, but all she says is, "Well, see folks know you're worth something. Tell 'em you're magic with machinery." Then, sagging into herself, she sets the car struggling back the way it came.

The boy she called Moss turns my way. Sun-faded hair hangs on his forehead, and his body is that kind of bony, long-muscle, tight-skin lanky that comes of scrabbling-hard work. Hurt or anger makes his face harsh.

He says—to himself or me, I can't tell which—"She knows there's nothin' for me home, and Pa didn't ask my company."

I hardly know what to answer. He's got troubles a lot bigger than mine if I understand right—his family has just broken apart and he's suddenly on his own. "I'm sorry."

The boy flushes. "It ain't your worry." Then he heads across the lot to where Joe is still sorting radiator caps.

I ache for him, just imagining...

"Hey, Moss! My name's Beatty," I yell, not stopping to

13

think why I want him to know. "Beatrice Anne Donnough. You hear?"

Back at the tourist court, I find Clo setting up her sewing machine. She's underneath it, doing something to the treadle. "There's Ovaltine waiting, angel," she tells me. "And cookies. Did you see your father? This thing's jammed…"

Then, turning, she catches sight of my face. "Beatty? What's wrong?"

"Everything," I tell her, explaining about the old car and its family, about Dad being so angry, about the woman pilot getting mad at Grif because the field wasn't clear.

I describe her and add, "Clo, she knew me, or knew Dad, anyway."

It's the kind of mystery we can usually talk about for hours, but now all Clo says is, "I've no idea who the woman is." My aunt seems distracted, and after a bit she walks down to the tourist court office. Through the window I see her at the telephone.

A pang goes though me as I realize she must be calling Grif. *Surely what I did wasn't enough to cause a problem for him?*

The fold-out sofa in the front room of our cabin has been made into a bed for me. It's night now, and I should be going to sleep, but instead I'm wide awake, thinking about the day.

I did my apologizing to Grif over supper, until finally he said, "Beatty, stop worrying about what's done. I don't think anything will come of it, anyway." He turned to Clo and gave her this sappy, silly look. "Water under the bridge, right, honey?"

14

Lovers' good humor, I guess. I laugh quietly myself now, remembering how nobody argued when I said I thought I'd go for a walk.

Through a window and shade open to any breeze, I watch the flash of the Hi-Way Tourist Court sign. Headlight beams swing in and out of a malt-shop lot across the road, and kids call good night to each other.

I hear a plane go overhead, probably the 10:35 mail flight that Grif had to go meet. It's a lonely sound, over the town but not part of it.

Abruptly I remember that lonely boy, Moss. Is he hearing it, too?

I hope Joe helped him somehow—told him, at least, someplace he could sleep.

Moss is one of the first people Clo and I see when we go into town the next morning to get cleaner for my dress.

We're walking down a block of nice old houses when I spot him pulling weeds from a rose bed.

"Clo," I say, "look yonder...I'm sure it's that boy I told you about, the one whose family left him."

"He didn't waste time finding work."

"Moss!" I call. "Moss!"

His head whips around, but when he sees me he gives a half wave and returns to the weeding.

I wonder if he was hoping it was his mother, or maybe a sister, come to ask him to change his mind.

I start to call out again, but Clo puts a hand on my arm. "Beatty," she says, "the person he's working for might not want him visiting, and besides, you don't know him."

———

15

Clo and I take our time finding the cleaning fluid. We poke into this store and that, Clo being almost as new to Muddy Springs as I am. In the dime store she picks out some yellow gingham to make curtains.

"For a tourist cabin?" I ask.

"I'm going to put in deep-enough hems that they ought to fit wherever we go." My aunt looks a little embarrassed, but proud, too. "I thought if we could always see our own curtains, it would help make all the motor courts we're living in feel like home. Since, as long as Grif's got this relief job, we won't really have a place of our own."

"But don't you like moving around? Thinking there might be something exciting waiting at the next place?"

Clo looks at me curiously. "Is there usually?"

"No. But I like knowing there might be. Anyway, it's not as though I'm leaving family, the way that boy's doing by staying here…"

I pause, seeing my aunt's smile lessen and hearing how my words must have sounded to her. "Of course," I amend, "you are family, especially you, and I'm always sorry to say good-bye. I just meant—"

"I know what you meant, Beatty. And I guess since it's true, we better both be glad you like moving around."

"But you don't?"

"It's not what I'd pick." Then she laughs. "I'm not Beatty, happy to be footloose!"

We find thread and a packet of rickrack on the notions counter, and Clo counts out change for her purchase. "So," she asks as we leave the store, "how was Waco this spring?"

"Good. The day I started back to school someone put a

WELCOME BEATTY sign on the trophy case, so it was the first thing I saw."

"Cupcakes to go with it?"

I shake my head, knowing Clo's reminding me of the send-off my class in San Antonio gave me when I left there in January.

I don't think my friends in either place have skipped giving me some kind of good-bye or hello once in all the time I've been making the midyear switch. Not any more than my teachers have missed reporting to each other exactly how far along I am in my textbooks.

Of course, the routine will be broken this fall, since I won't be returning to San Antonio. Grandpa's dead, and with Clo married and moved away there's no one there for me to go to. The plan was for me to stay on a few extra months in Dallas with Fanny, enroll in North Dallas High, but now that she's trying to figure out what to do herself...

As though Clo reads my mind, she says, "Beatty, we'll work out something."

"I know. You guys"—I mean my aunts—"always do."

By this time we're again passing the house where we saw Moss, but now the yard is empty except for a woman in a lawn swing. Before Clo can stop me, I go over.

"Why, no," the woman tells me, "I don't know where the boy's gone. I gave him breakfast in return for cleaning out my garden, but that's all the chores I had."

"Beatty," Clo tells me, "I know you mean well, but you can't make a strange boy your concern."

17

4

BACK AT THE tourist court, Clo stands at the open door of the icebox and says, "For pity's sake, now Grif really *did* forget his lunch."

"Maybe he'll come get it," I suggest, hopeful I won't have to make that hot bike ride again and realizing I will.

I don't intend to stop at Joe's Texas Auto Parts, but Joe's out front when I ride up. He calls, "That airport still lost?"

"No, sir," I answer, veering over. "I found it and guess I will again, if it's not moved." Then I ask if Moss has been by.

"What for? I told him I hardly got work enough for me, and sure none extra." He looks at me sharply. "What's your interest?"

"None, really. I just saw how his folks took off yesterday. It was sad."

"He's a wandering boy now."

A wandering boy. There's thousands on the roads, and Moss is just one more.

"When you talked to him, did he say...I mean, where was he even going to stay?"

"No telling," Joe says, "though I did mention an old boxcar up by the bluff, dry anyway and empty, far as I know. That ain't saying he's gone to it."

I'm about to leave when Joe tells me to wait while he fetches a few peaches. "Take these along. Just in case you find him."

"I'm not looking—"

"I said, 'in case.' Now get goin' 'fore your plane leaves without you."

"But I'm not—" Then I see Joe's teasing again. "One day," I tell him. "One day I *will* get a plane ride."

Biking up Airfield Road—no more shortcuts for me—I study a low smudge of reddish brown in the not-too-far distance. That's got to be the bluff Joe meant, the only rise visible in all this flat land.

A vehicle overtakes me, a little open roadster trailing dust clouds and noise. It brakes to a halt, and the driver waits for me to catch up. It's Gold Lightning, I realize after a moment. Somehow she looked better in her flying suit than she does in the sprigged cotton dress she's now wearing, an outfit that seems way too dainty for her.

Though, to be fair, if I hadn't seen her yesterday I probably wouldn't think that.

"You," she says, "Donnough's daughter. What do people call you?"

"Beatty. For Beatrice."

"You going out to the airport again?"

"Yes."

"Well, do something for me. Give this to Kenzie and let him know I've got a pupil coming in at five o'clock, so I'll need my plane ready by then."

Hardly giving me a chance to take the leaflet she holds out, she makes a dirt-spitting three-point turn and starts off. Then, fifty feet away, she stops again. This time she backs up until she's even with me.

"Beatty..."

She seems uncertain about what she wants to say, and impatient, too. With herself for being indecisive, is my guess, considering how up to now about all I've heard from her are orders.

"Beatty," she repeats, "what I said yesterday—I hope you are learning good sense..."

It's such a strange thing to say, and so ill mannered that I'm tempted to snap off, *No*.

But I can see from how her face flushes that she doesn't mean it rudely: She's just not as good asking a personal question, whatever her reason, as she was demanding to know what a fool was doing in her landing path.

So I nod, intending to ask why she wants to know and how yesterday she put Dad and me together.

Gold Lightning doesn't give me a chance. "Good," she says, driving off, leaving me to chew dust and think her interest really does seem odd.

It's strange enough I'll ask my dad to explain the next time he comes through Muddy Springs. Assuming that by then he's calmed down.

And I hope it won't just make him angry again.

Grif's got three people to check in for the afternoon flight, an unanticipated crowd for Muddy Springs.

I listen for a moment while Grif explains to a woman that, no, he is not being fresh by weighing her and her luggage. "Airline regulations require me to figure load allowances and balance. With full flights there's not a lot of leeway."

Another passenger interrupts. "Ma'am, I've flown many times, and there's always some weigh-in. If our plane's to get in the air, there's just so many pounds—us and fuel and cargo—it can carry."

"Young man," the woman says, "I understand that. But I assure you my suitcase is not more than the allowed thirty pounds, and as for my person..."

I put Grif's lunch where he'll see it, wave the leaflet, and point toward the hangar.

Kenzie has the *Gold Lightning* plane pulled in the shade just inside. He's working in the forward seat of its cockpit, and judging from the way he's talking to himself—just this side of outright swearing—I guess he's having a hard time with something. Suddenly his arm jerks back and a tangle of webbing sails my way. "Gol *durn* it!"

Turning, he exclaims, "You! Beatty, isn't it?"

"Yes."

"Well, Beatty, pick that piece of junk up and toss it away. I don't want to see the thing again."

"OK, but I've brought you something from the pilot."

Ignoring the leaflet I reach up to him, Kenzie climbs down from the plane and gets the webbing himself. "Blockhead who designed this ought to be shot," he says. "No proper connections, doesn't fit, probably won't be no use, nohow."

"Do you want this?" I ask, offering the paper again.

"What? Put it on the workbench."

Certainly, Mr. Kenzie. You're welcome, Mr. Kenzie.

Reading as I carry it over, I see the leaflet is instructions for installing what sounds like that webbing he was swearing about. I briefly enjoy thinking, *Well, Mr. Kenzie, you can just find that out for yourself.*

But I can't be quite that mean spirited. Almost despite myself, I say, "Kenzie, this paper might help with what you're fixing."

An hour later I leave the airport, still uncertain just how Kenzie roped me into reading those instructions to him step by step. Or how I ended up wrist-deep in kerosene and grease again, sorting what he calls valves from valve springs and connecting rods and pistons.

"What's this all for?" I asked.

"Spare parts for overhauling engines, of course," he told me, with a look that dared me to ask what an engine is.

And so instead I asked about Gold Lightning.

"I don't know much but her name, Annie Boudreau," Kenzie answered. "Been giving flying lessons over in Fort Worth, and now she's decided to expand her business to Muddy Springs a couple of days a week. Even brought a car over."

"She didn't sound like Fort Worth."

"Yankee, I'd say. You keeping those parts straight?"

"Yes, Kenzie," I answered, and kept at the work until it was done.

And now I have to decide which way to go.

I know I should return to town. Clo's expecting me.

But there's the peaches in my bicycle basket....Just how far away is that bluff, anyway?

Past the airport, the road runs straight north. I'm not good at judging distances, but I suppose I've gone a mile or so when the bluff suddenly ceases to be a distant smudge and becomes, instead, a reachable line of gullied rock. A ribbon of brush and scrub oak meandering along its base shows where there's a creek.

As I get closer I see it's almost dried up.

So now where do I go?

A sound like a door banging comes from somewhere fairly close. I search, at first not seeing anything in the heavy brush, then making out a line too straight to be natural.

It turns out to be not a boxcar like Joe said but an old caboose, half falling apart, glass missing from its windows. *How*, I wonder, *did it ever get out here?*

I'm about to call a greeting when noise in the undergrowth startles me. Whirling about, I spot an armadillo digging through dead leaves.

"He won't hurt," Moss, suddenly next to me, says. And then his voice gets an edge. "What'd you come after?"

"Moss, you gave me a worse start than that animal did."

"I asked, what do you want?"

"To give you these peaches. There's no call to be rude."

"I ain't hungry."

"Then feed them to the blasted armadillo." Annoyed at him for making me feel foolish, I toss the peaches on the ground. One hits something sharp and splits open.

"Hey," Moss says, lunging after it, "you shouldn' throwed 'em." Then he yells, "Ouch!" and cradles his hand.

"Cactus spine?" I ask.

"I guess." He probes a thumb joint, grimacing. "It's splintered off."

"Let me see."

I turn his hand to get the light. It's all calluses layered over ground-in grease. "You got tweezers? Or anything sharp?"

"My pocketknife's inside," he says.

I start toward the caboose, but he tells me, "Never mind. I'll fix it later."

"Not without gouging yourself, unless you're left-handed as well as right."

I pull open the door. Opposite, light shines in a rectangle where another door used to be.

The inside's a mess, all but one end, and I realize that Moss has started cleaning up from that side. It's been swept—the trash, anyway—and a makeshift seat's pulled up to a counter. One bunk along the wall looks straighter than the rest, too, so I guess that's where Moss slept.

"You've got this part looking almost like a room!" I exclaim. "I had a place I fixed up once, an old storm shelter no one was using, and I did just like you've done, set up a pallet and a place to eat, and…"

My voice trails off as I realize the difference: That was play and this isn't.

"Here," Moss says, getting his knife. His face and his voice both tell me he's embarrassed, and I look around for something easy to talk about.

"Find any treasures yet? What's that stuff?" I point to dials and wire and coils heaped in a pile. "Is it from some kind of radio?"

"Maybe," Moss answers. "Look, help if you're going to, and then you better leave. I got to see about a janitor's job at the picture show, anyways."

I take a last look around. *Does he really think he can live out here?*

I SEE CLO'S STRUNG a clothesline beside our cabin and is hanging out my dress, all scrubbed clean.

"Hi there," she says. "I was wondering where you got to."

"I went exploring."

A black sedan pulls in the lot, and the woman driving it goes in the office and then pulls up to our place. "Yoohoo," she calls, getting out. "Mrs. Langston?"

Extending a hand, my aunt says, "I'm Clo Langston."

"Bee Granger. My husband, Ben—he's a director on the airport board—said I should come make sure you're settled in OK." She drops into a lawn chair, a bit breathless. "I would of come sooner, but this heat…"

"This is my niece, Beatty," Clo tells her. "May I offer you some iced tea, Mrs. Granger? Beatty, will you please bring us some?"

When I come out with the drinks, the woman is saying to Clo, "Now, I wouldn't want it to get back to Mr. Granger I told you, but I understand that the man your husband is filling in for may not be coming back until fall. If at all." She leans closer to my aunt. "Women trouble."

"What kind of women trouble?" I ask.

"Beatty!" Clo scolds me. Then the import of it hits her. "Mrs. Granger, do you think Grif might stay on for a while, then?"

"That's what the airline told Mr. Granger."

I slip into a chair and listen to the two of them go on, Clo trying to find out more about the Muddy Springs job and her visitor intent on the failings of the absent station manager. Then Clo asks me, "Beatty, isn't it that boy?"

I follow her gaze to where Moss is walking along the highway toward town.

"Who is he?" Mrs. Granger asks, her voice faintly disapproving. "Surely he's not from around here?"

"No," I answer. "He's just arrived and is looking for work."

"I see." Mrs. Granger shifts her gaze to the malt shop. "Have you investigated the Mirage yet, Beatty? I understand that's where the young people gather."

"I figured so. I heard the voices last night."

The conversation turns to various Muddy Springs women's groups, and eventually, when there's a chance, I say, "If I may be excused, maybe I will go across the street."

The Mirage has a palm tree and blue lagoon painted on its stucco front, and music from a record player fairly throbs through lattice-shaded windows. It's the kind of place you don't enter so much as plunge into.

Which is what I am trying to decide if I really want to do when two girls walk up behind me. "You going in or just looking, honey?" one asks, a redhead like Clo.

"Going in, I suppose."

The place is filled, kids talking at tables, a few couples dancing, a soda jerk working the long ice-cream counter.

"You're new here, aren't you?" the redhead asks. I tell her I am, and my name, and she says she's Julie Elise Armstrong. "Come on," she says. "Meet the gang."

First, though, we order sodas, Julie Elise talking nonstop both to me and to the young man who waits on us.

"I didn't think I'd seen you before," she says to me. "And besides, I was sure you'd just come to town because your face was a giveaway, with that Do-I-open-the-door? look. I know the feeling. I get it every time I'm new in a place myself, which is about every year, because...

"Rudy, are you going to make us those sodas or not?

"So, Beatty, are you living in Muddy Springs or just visiting? We should get you down to—"

"Julie Elise," the other girl breaks in, "stop babbling and come sit down."

At pushed-together tables I meet another half dozen kids. Names come too fast for me to get them all straight, but I attach Leila to Julie Elise's friend and Henry and Milton to two of the boys.

"When did you get here?" Henry asks, and I tell him just yesterday morning, on a bus from Dallas.

Julie Elise has introduced me as Beatty, but when Milton asks, "Hey, Dallas, do you dance?" I know what I'm going to be called as long as I'm in Muddy Springs.

"Sure," I answer.

We make space for ourselves between other dancing couples just as the music ends, and while we wait for the record to change, Milton tells me he plays football for Muddy Springs High. "It keeps me busy in the fall," he says. "And of course I'm a workingman, got to clerk Saturdays at the hardware store to support the old jalopy."

Close my eyes and he could be any boy I know in Dallas or Waco or San Antonio.

"That's nice," I say.

I stay at the Mirage a good while, though, grateful for the friendly welcome.

The only awkward moment comes when Julie Elise suddenly spots the grease I haven't quite got out from under my fingernails. "What *have* you been doing, Dallas?" she asks.

"Helping the airfield mechanic." I give some details to explain, but I stop when I see I'm telling more than anybody wants to know.

Soon after, I find an excuse to leave.

Crossing the highway to the tourist court, I'm surprised to see that Grif's automobile is parked in front of the cabin. Then I spot Clo and him roasting hot dogs on sticks over a small charcoal fire. They're holding hands, but they quit that when I call, "Hi, I'm home."

"I was just coming to get you," Clo says.

"It didn't look that way to me," I answer. Then, because they both seem so embarrassed, I feel bad about teasing.

Clo says that supper's early because Grif has to get back to the airport to check in some air express.

"Kenzie says you gave him a hand today," Grif tells me.

"Just read to him, mainly. He sure can be grumpy."

"He'd rather be flying planes than fixing them, I'd guess," Grif says. "But that bad leg's got him permanently grounded."

By this time the traffic out on the highway is increasing. A lot of it is kids leaving the malt shop. Milton sees us and taps out a shave-and-a-haircut-two-bits rhythm on his car horn, which makes Clo raise her eyebrows. "Promising?"

"Nope," I answer, just as I glimpse Moss walking along the edge of the road from the direction of town. His shoulders are hunched, his head down.

"I guess he didn't get the theater job," I say.

Grif asks, "Who? That boy? No wonder, if he went asking for it looking like that."

"You'd look shabby, too," I say, "if you were living all alone in an abandoned railroad car and you didn't have a thing to your name, not even soap." I stop, realizing Clo and Grif are staring at me in surprise, and Clo asks, "Beatty, how do you know...?"

But then she flings herself out of the lawn chair and snaps a dead branch from a scrawny tree. "Oh, for heaven's sake. Beatty, I told you...Here," she says, handing me the branch. "Put on another frankfurter."

Then she walks down to the road. "Moss?" she calls. "I'm Beatty's aunt. Come join us?"

Moss isn't like any other boy I know. Not that any of the ones I do know are rich. It's just he's the first I've ever known who's truly poor.

He has good manners, though. He's got bad grammar and says *not no* like a country boy, but he also says *sir* and *ma'am*. And when Grif mentions an automobile problem, Moss talks about exhaust manifolds and differentials and never misses a syllable.

The two of them end up under the car, their legs sticking out and their voices and experimental knocks on various metal parts carrying Clo's and my way.

Moss doesn't leave until Grif does, Grif offering him a ride as far as the airport.

"He seems a nice boy," Clo says afterward. Then she adds,

"But don't get involved with him, Beatty. He's got no family, apparently—not given what you saw—and who knows where he's from."

"Good heavens, Clo! Moss is just a friend. Hardly that, even. Though I am glad you gave him supper."

6

THE NEXT MORNING, as soon as Clo leaves for a meeting and luncheon Mrs. Granger's invited her to, I put together a few things for Moss: a wedge of cornbread, two deviled eggs, and a slice of watermelon. Also a bar of soap.

The girls I met yesterday are going in the Mirage as I pull my bike onto the highway, and Julie Elise calls, "Hey, Dallas!"

"Hey!" I call back, but I don't stop. "I'll try to catch you this afternoon."

It's so late I'm afraid Moss might have already left to go job hunting, but he's out front of the old caboose when I get there.

"I told you I don't need handouts," he says.

"And I don't need ingratitude. I'll wait while you wash up."

Moss looks like he's trying to decide whether to challenge me. Then he smiles a bit. "You wait inside, then. The only water I got's out here."

He's done a lot of straightening since yesterday. A holey blanket, tied back to let in light and fresh air, has replaced the missing door. Almost all the mess has been hauled to a pile out back.

Only that tangle of parts is left. They're spread across the counter.

"Tell me…," I say, as I hear him step inside. His hair's wet and his face scrubbed—*Why, he's not bad looking*— "What are you doing with all this stuff?"

"Trying to figure out what it is."

"You think you can make something of it?"

Moss shrugs. "I don't know. I wish I could get it clean enough to see what all's here, anyways."

"Moss," I tell him, "one thing I do know is where there's stuff for cleaning metal."

We walk together as far as the airport, sharing the lunch, Moss wheeling my bike along. He flat-out refuses to go in with me, though, saying he won't ask for things he can't pay for.

"The mechanic owes me," I say. "I did some work for him."

That brings Moss's head snapping around, and for the first time he looks at me as if he's trying to see just who I am. "I never knowed a girl to do shop work."

I'm tempted to let him stay impressed, but something makes me be honest. "Actually," I admit, "what I did was clean and sort parts."

"Still…Anyways, have him give you something for yourself."

"Moss," I tell him, "what I ask for is my business. You go on to town if you want."

I find Kenzie cleaning the windshield of a small private plane. His one hand's polishing glass, the other gently resting on the gleaming body.

"Kenzie," I say before really thinking, "you must miss flying."

And he says, "I do, Beatty. There is nothing in this world like it." Then he catches himself. "Nothing that's more work, either. You come to make yourself useful?"

"No. I came to ask for a little kerosene. Though if you need me..."

It takes Kenzie about two seconds to fetch some ammonia water and get me up in the cockpit washing dials.

"What's this one?" I ask, and he calls it an altimeter. He says it's to tell how high up a plane is flying.

"And this?"

"Don't you know a compass? And there's the fuel gauge, and that one nearest your hand, it's the airspeed indicator."

I'm repeating the words to myself, *altimeter, compass, fuel gauge, air...*, when I realize Kenzie, down on the floor now and draining gasoline into a steel drum, is asking a question. "How about you? You like flyin'?"

"I've never been, but I know I'm going to like it," I tell him.

"Never?" he asks. Peering my way, he kind of starts. "Beatty, you look so much like your mother up there I almost called you Lindsey."

"You knew my mother?"

"And you without any notion what flying's like! It'd be funny if it weren't so sorry. Lindsey Donnough's daughter earthbound!"

"You knew my mother?" I repeat, incredulous.

Nobody ever tells me they knew my mother. She was from someplace up north, New York or near there, without people of her own, and Dad didn't bring her to Texas until just before she died. Even my aunts didn't know her except as a person dying.

That's how, all my life, I've thought of her, just a woman too weak to talk, much less care for her year-old daughter.

But now Kenzie's telling me, "We worked together a bit back in the old days. I remember once we was delivering a couple of planes to an exhibition—a new idea, flying planes to where they was needed instead of sending them on a train. Anyway, we was supposed to be flying tandem, but with Lindsey that meant chasing after her—"

"My mother was a *pilot*?"

"Huh! After the war was over and she got that little Jenny biplane of hers—part of the surplus the government sold off— she flew like she had her own wings."

"A *pilot*?"

Kenzie jerks around to face me, and now his voice is the one disbelieving. "You mean you didn't know?"

I shake my head.

"Well, ask your dad. And ask him to get you a seat pass from the company, too. Lindsey Donnough's daughter never been up in a plane. Sinful."

As I go searching for Grif, I think how I *have* asked my dad to take me flying. He's just never been any more willing to discuss his reasons for saying no than he's been willing to answer questions about my mother.

I've heard Dad say, "There's no use talking, Beatty. Your mother's gone," so many times that I have about stopped asking. Especially now that I'm old enough to realize some of the possible reasons for his silence, other than him just missing her:

that maybe they'd fallen out of love or something had gone wrong between them.

But that doesn't excuse Dad for not telling me the *facts* of her.

I catch up to my uncle as he's rolling a drum of heavy cable out to one of the landing-field lights. He's sweaty faced and provoked, muttering about the lights needing more attention than he knows how to give.

"Grif, Kenzie just told me my mother was a pilot. Did you know that?"

"Your mother? No. Here, hold this clip."

"It's what Kenzie said. He wouldn't make up a thing like that."

"I don't know anything about your mother, Beatty. Ask Clo."

"I'm on my way to."

But Grif tells me there's no point hurrying, since Clo telephoned from the luncheon to say she was staying on to play cards.

I don't remember Moss and his radio parts until Kenzie waves me down as I'm getting my bike. "Thought you wanted these," he says, handing me a pint of kerosene and a bag of rags. "Fair pay for fair work. Next time, put away what you use."

At least pedaling back to the bluff gives me something to put my muscles to while my mind puzzles over what I've learned. *My mom flew.*

My mother! Nobody's mother is a pilot.

The question I can't imagine an answer to, though, is *Why didn't anyone—why didn't Dad—tell me?*

———

I leave the cleaning stuff on the caboose step, where Moss can't miss seeing it, and I start back. The early-afternoon sun is all pulsing heat, and my stomach is grumbling because I haven't had lunch, except for the little bit I ate to keep Moss company.

Nearing the airport, I see Grif up on the terminal roof doing something to a floodlight, and of course, from up there he sees me.

"Beatty!" he calls. "Hey, Beatty!"

There's no way I can go by without stopping, but I'm saved from questions about where I've been by the arrival of a car.

Grif looks at his watch. "That can't be a passenger for the westbound plane already!" he exclaims, hurrying down a ladder. "I should have had the rest rooms cleaned and the weather report in by now..."

"You clean bathrooms?"

"Beatty, do you see anyone else out here to do it?"

I trail him inside, where he's just getting a mop and pail from a janitor's closet when the radio's loudspeaker calls Muddy Springs.

"Now what?" Grif asks, heading to the operations room.

I listen as he talks to a pilot flying a feeder route, a guy who got off course and then made a forced landing in a farm field way to the north.

Grif asks, "Anyone hurt?...Thank goodness...Yeah, I'll get fuel out to you once our afternoon plane's off the ground."

Then he adds, "You've got *what*? Well, don't let 'em cook."

As Grif signs off, a passenger comes in the terminal juggling belongings and looking for someone to help him.

Grif says, "Beatty, I've got to let that pilot's outfit know about the downed plane. Please tell that passenger I'll be with him in just a minute, and then go ask Kenzie to get the service truck ready."

"Can I go with you?" I ask, watching Kenzie run gasoline into the tank on his truck. "Out to the plane, I mean?"

"If your uncle says. Here, hang up this nozzle."

Grif, coiling a length of rope, says he doesn't see why not. "Just stay out of the way of any passengers. They tend to get agitated over unplanned stops."

"Why did the plane land out in the country?"

"Coming out the Panhandle, the pilot got surprised by a thunderstorm and had to fly around both his scheduled stop and an emergency field. Then his fuel wouldn't stretch quite enough to get him here."

"What's the rope for?"

Grif glances at Kenzie. "In case the cargo needs walking."

"Dogs again?" Kenzie asks.

"That's what it sounded like."

Driving north, Kenzie and I come on Moss trudging up the washboard road toward the bluff.

"Can we take him along?" I ask Kenzie. "He's the friend I got the solvent for."

"This ain't a tour bus."

"Maybe he can help with whatever needs walking."

Slowing to a stop, Kenzie grumbles, "In the old days, an airplane passenger didn't get coddled, and he sure didn't cart his pets along. A mail bag on his lap maybe, and another likely under his feet...and that's *if* he could get a spare seat in an open-cockpit plane..."

Kenzie raises his voice to reach Moss. "Well? You gettin' in?"

The plane is a small, single-engine aircraft, all streamlined and fast looking with high, cantilevered wings. Only now it's resting empty in a cotton field, seeming about as forlorn as the three passengers sitting on suitcases under the shade of one of those wings.

Squawks and yowls and an intermittent "Hello, hello" come from crates piled under the other wing. Nearby, a man is poking among spindly plants and calling, "Millie? Here, Mill. Here, girl."

"Uh-oh," Kenzie says. "You kids can help."

I check the crates first, saying, "Hello, hello," to a parrot in one of them. Stenciled on the crate's side is COLONEL BO MARSHALL AND HIS ACTING ANIMALS, STARS OF THE SILVER SCREEN.

Movie stars!

"Hello, hello," says that particular star.

Millie turns out to be a trained dog that took off after a jackrabbit. "When I get that durn mutt back, I just may turn her into rabbit stew herself," Colonel Marshall says. "She's not so big a star I won't do it."

Kenzie begins fueling the plane, and the pilot, reloading animal crates, tells the passengers they'll be leaving in a jiffy.

A moment later, though, as gasoline splashes the dry ground, Kenzie says, "You better rethink that *jiffy*. With fuel leaking somehow, this plane's ain't going noplace today."

The passengers murmur in protest, and Colonel Marshall

says, "But at least my birds and that dog *must* be on the set tomorrow. In Hollywood."

"Now, folks," says the pilot, "we'll get you all where you're going as fast as possible. And you'll get a night in Muddy Springs on the airline. Dinner included."

"And how will we get to Muddy Springs?" someone asks.

They ride in and on Kenzie's truck. The two women crowd in the front seat, and the pilot perches on the running boards. The other men sit in the back, keeping tight hold on the animal crates Moss has helped rope down.

"What about Moss and me?" I ask Kenzie.

"You see room?" He hands us a couple of water bottles before getting behind the steering wheel. "You two wait here. Beatty, your uncle or me'll be back soon as we can."

"And keep an eye out for my dog," Colonel Marshall adds. He turns to the pilot. "If that animal is not in the studio on time, I will expect your airline to pay for a replacement."

7

$\mathcal{Y}$OU'D THINK WE'D see her," I tell Moss as we walk parallel rows of cotton searching for Millie. "These plants are hardly big enough to hide behind. And why's she hiding?"

"You want me to read a dog's mind?" Moss asks. "I once had a hound what wouldn't do nothing all day but watch water drip out a cistern."

My stomach's really making noise now. "Let's check in the airplane for some food," I suggest. "The passengers get box lunches—maybe someone didn't eat."

Moss looks like he can't believe I didn't mention food earlier, if I knew it was a possibility.

The plane's door is standing open above a hanging step, and Moss hurries to climb inside, grabbing one edge of the doorway and yelling how hot the sun's made it. Then he puts out a hand to haul me up.

"Thanks," I gasp, as scorching air whams against my chest. "This place is an oven."

Moss wastes no time. When he doesn't find any uneaten lunches, he goes though a bag of trash, pulling out empty cardboard boxes and used napkins. "Here's a sandwich still wrapped," he says.

The plane's not very big—just two seats on the door side and three opposite. I look in the pocket behind each, hoping maybe Moss has overlooked something better than throwaways. And in the pocket behind one seat, I do find one of those traveler's packets that passengers are given. It's got a strip map of the route, cotton for ears, a little ammonia inhalant for airsickness, and chewing gum.

"I found gum," I call.

Toward the front I come across a full vacuum bottle. "And lemonade."

Then I peer into the cockpit and up through an open hatch that lets hot air out but also lets the sun pour in.

Just then I hear a sound...at least I think I do...like a soft whine....

"Moss!" I shout. "I found Millie."

She's wedged between the cockpit seat and the floor pedals, a small black-and-white Border collie that right now appears half-dead.

"Hey," I reassure her, putting a hand on her side. "You're going to be OK."

But she's breathing in shallow pants, and her body and nose feel way too warm.

"Come on," Moss says. "We best get her outside."

Millie is heavier than she looks, thirty-five or forty pounds of limp weight, but between the two of us we get her off the plane. Moss offers her some warm water from one of the bottles Kenzie left us, but she doesn't even try to drink.

Then I think of the lemonade, which might be cooler. I get Moss to pour a little into my cupped hands. "Come on, Millie," I say. "Poor pup...Moss, why do you think she went back inside?"

Moss shakes his head. "No tellin', but I think we ought to eat." He takes out part of the sandwich, holding it so I can take a couple of bites, and then he has some himself.

For a long moment Millie lies where we've put her, stretched out in the shade of the plane. Then, with a huge effort, she raises her head enough to lap down the lemonade.

"Good girl," I tell her. "Good girl. Moss, maybe she wants more."

While I try to get her to drink, Moss wets down his shirt and lays it over her and works on keeping the pads of her feet moist and cool.

It must take Millie the better part of a half hour to get the rest of the lemonade down, but she finishes it standing up, and by then her body's not so over-hot. I'm saying "Good girl" again when she snatches what's left of the sandwich from Moss's pocket and skitters out of reach.

"Hey!" Moss shouts, but he doesn't come even close to catching her. She runs, halts long enough to rip into the wrapping, and then runs some more.

"Millie," Moss calls. "Stop. Stay. Bring that back. Beatty, help catch her."

But I'm laughing too hard to do anything but watch as Millie gobbles it.

Moss sinks down next to me. "I was counting on that!"

"You were!" I tell him. "Me, too!"

Millie cocks her head like she's trying to understand. And then she very carefully picks up a shred of waxed paper and brings it to me. She goes back and gets another and then another, until every bit of it is in a neat pile in my lap.

Dropping into a crouch, her amber eyes intent on my face, she thumps her tail.

"What do you want me to say, Millie?" I ask her. "You just stole our only food!"

Thump. Thump.

"All right. So you cleaned up, too. OK. Good girl. Now are you happy? Good girl!"

Thump, thump, thump, thump, thump, thump.

"Millie don't sound like much of a movie star's name," Moss says.

"Maybe it's short for something like Mademoiselle Millicent," I answer.

It's early evening, a little cooler now that the sun's going down. We're perched on one of the plane's plywood wings, our legs dangling over the edge. Millie, who insisted on being hauled up through the cockpit hatch with us, is lying with her head on my knee and her tail thumping against Moss.

"That looks like the airfield," I say as, way in the distance, lights come on one after another. "I guess somebody will be coming for us soon. Or they better be, since Clo's probably long back at the tourist court. I hope Grif got a message to her."

"I was wondering about that," Moss says. "Why that's where you all are living."

I explain how Grif's job is to move from one airfield to another on vacation relief.

"So you all will be goin' soon?" Moss asks, and I'm pleased that he sounds disappointed.

44

"It may be Grif will work here all summer, anyway."

"And you'll stay?"

"I guess."

And then I go on to tell him why I'm here in Muddy Springs at all: how I live with Clo and my dad's two older sisters turnabout, and would be in Dallas now except for a damaging windstorm. "Aunt Fanny says there's no telling when she'll move back home or reopen the lunchroom she runs on the porch. And my other aunt can't have me just now."

I'm searching for a way to ask Moss about his own family when he says, "I guess you saw my folks don't have much. The bank took our place."

"But I thought your mother was returning home."

"Movin' in with relations."

"And you didn't want to go with her?"

"Nah, I'd hate movin' around, askin' this 'un and that to take us in. I'd rather be settled in a place of my own, even a railroad car." Moss halts, realizing, I suppose, I must think he's criticizing how I live.

"That's OK," I tell him. "I guess people just want what they're used to. And I like moving around, not feeling too committed."

Said like that, our differences seem huge, and for a few moments we don't talk more but just listen to the land around us. It's full of sound, crickets and night birds, slitherings and brushings and twigs snapping.

Then Moss says, "I asked Ma to write me at the post office here and say how it goes."

"Do you think she will? I mean, would she be honest whether things are good or bad?"

When Moss doesn't answer right away I say, "I'm sorry. I had no right to ask."

"It's OK. Yeah, Ma would tell me."

There's something in the tone of Moss's voice that makes me turn to see his expression. I wonder if my question's just reminded him how bad off he and his folks are. The dusk doesn't let me see well enough to know, though, and the odd note is gone when Moss asks, "How about your people, Beatty? Ain't they honest with you?"

"Yes," I say. "That is, as far as I know. Except I'm finding they leave things out. Moss…"

And suddenly I'm telling him all I learned today, what Kenzie said about my mother being a pilot, and how it seems so unbelievable that no one ever told me.

"Do you remember her at all?" Moss asks.

"No. I just know what I've been told, that when Dad showed up at my grandparents' with me and my mother, she was so sick with pneumonia she couldn't talk. She died right after, and then Grandmother died—maybe got sick from my mother, though I don't know that. It was late in the fall after my first birthday."

"And that's when you started moving around?"

"Pretty much. Clo was a kid still, and she and I were sent to her and Dad's big sisters, who were already grown and married. Once Clo was old enough to watch me, we started spending summers with my grandfather. And then she started staying on with him for the school year and it was just me going to my other aunts' for the winter."

"Complicated," Moss says.

"It worked."

We fall silent again as I think about those early years, how I first was scared of all that moving and then got glad for it. Like I told Clo, I enjoy knowing something exciting may be waiting out front. And behind…well, behind is for entanglements, where you leave problems when you move on.

Moss breaks into my thoughts, asking, "Beatty, was your ma with the airline, too?"

"I don't think so, Moss. I don't think there were airlines back then. But she was good. Kenzie said she was such a good pilot that she'd try to climb to the sun."

"A teacher showed me a picture of that once."

"A picture of my mother?"

"No." Moss laughs. "Of this winged person flying near the sun. I disremember his name…"

Icarus. I know the story. He flew too close to the sun and his wings melted.

Just then a car's headlights come in sight. "Looks like Grif's the one who's had to rescue us, on top of doing everything else," I tell Moss.

And that's when I get my idea.

"Moss, maybe you can work at the airport! Grif's got way too much to do. Ask him if you can't help with stuff like mopping up and carrying bags. Just for food, I mean, until you can get a paying job."

Moss takes a moment before answering, "I'll think on it."

8

SOON WE'RE IN my uncle's car, bouncing over the field toward the road. He's come full of apologies for being so long—"one thing after another"—and, thank goodness, brings us a box of crackers. I take a good stack and hand the rest back to Moss, who's in the rear seat with Millie. I figure the two of them can work out for themselves who gets how much.

"I guess Colonel Bo Marshall will be happy to get his dog back," I tell my uncle.

"Not him," Grif answers. "He caught the evening train, said he was done trusting airplanes. And he said if Millie showed up, we should feed her to the coyotes."

"You wouldn't—"

"No. But I can't say I have any idea what we can do with her. You've seen the tourist court rules. 'No pets allowed.'"

"But we can't just leave her on her own."

It's Moss, of course, who ends up with her, pending his finding a way to keep her fed. We stop near the bluff where the caboose is, and Moss gets out, telling Millie, "Come on, girl."

She stays put, looking uncertainly from him to me until I

give her a little push and add, "Go on, Mill. Moss'll take good care of you."

She jumps down then and goes with Moss. He starts off, calling back, "Good night, now. Thank you for the ride. Beatty, I'll think on your idea."

Grif and I don't leave the airport until after the night mail plane's come and gone, and by the time we get back to the tourist court Clo's asleep. She's left an "I love you two" note on the table, along with sliced meat loaf and rice pudding.

"I'm too weary to eat," Grif says, heading for the bedroom. And a little while later, when I tiptoe through on my way to wash up, he's already snoring.

Clo, though, whispers, "Good night, Beatty."

"Good night." Then I turn her way. "Clo? Are you awake enough we can talk?"

"Oh, angel," Clo says, sounding as if she'd rather sleep. Nevertheless, she slips into a robe and whispers, "Let's go in the other room."

"Some hot milk tea?" she asks, mixing half water and half milk in a saucepan. She holds a lit match to one of the stove burners and opens the gas jet. "Beatty, is this just girl talk or do you have something particular on your mind?"

"My mother," I answer. "Why didn't anybody tell me she used to fly?"

Clo looks surprised. "Did she?"

"That's what Kenzie says. Don't I have a right to know about her?"

"Of course. But, Beatty, I doubt I have anything to say that you haven't already heard."

"Tell me again."

"What?" Clo asks, coming to sit opposite me. "That your father was roaming around the country making exhibition flights for an airplane manufacturer when he met your mother? The first we learned of her was a postcard Collin sent saying the next time he got home he'd be bringing a bride who'd be a surprise to us all. Just after that the United States got into the war, and instead of returning to Texas, Collin signed up in the new Army Air Service."

"Where did my mother go? With him?"

"I don't know. We wrote and asked if she wanted to come down to us. Our letters never got answered. Beatty, no one even told us when you were born."

Clo gets up abruptly. Snapping the gas jet handle to Off, she says, "Look at this. I've gone and scalded the milk. I swear... Beatty, Collin is my brother and your father and I love him, but I can't forgive him for that, for not telling us you were born. Now, where is that sugar?"

"Here," I say, handing it to her. "Did you mind so much? You were pretty young."

Clo laughs at that, an embarrassed little sound. "Nine. I suppose I had half a crush on my glamorous big brother—and him not passing along such important news seemed a kind of betrayal." The smile goes away. "Besides, I was old enough to see how much my parents were hurt. It didn't make sense. Collin had always been..."

Clo pauses to choose her words. "Kind of the joyful noise in our house, barging in and out with friends when he was younger. Then sending silly notes from flying school, and afterward from this place or that—California, Missouri, New York. Only, after that one postcard...it was as though he chose to drop out of our lives."

She fills our cups and hands me one. "Here, see if this is sweet enough. I still don't understand what could have made Collin change so." Clo seems to catch herself. "Beatty, I apologize. I have no business talking about your father this way, even if he is my brother. And if your mother was a pilot, I never heard."

"Well, I'm going to ask Dad the first chance I get. Next week, maybe, if he comes for my birthday."

Clo says, "Beatty, I don't want you disappointed...but your father isn't much for talking about things he doesn't want to discuss."

"I know that," I tell her. "But I'm not much for being put off, either."

Which makes my aunt smile. "That's something I found out long ago!" She blows across her cup and sips. "Now, is that all that's on your mind?"

"Actually...Clo, do you think country boys have to always stay country boys, or can they change?"

My aunt's answer is a long, protesting groan. "Beatty...!"

We talk so late that Clo lets me sleep in the next morning. The 9:45 eastbound plane overhead wakes me up, and I'm still having breakfast when Julie Elise and Leila walk in.

"An easy life, girl," Leila teases. "What happened to you yesterday? You find someplace more interesting than the Mirage?"

Julie Elise doesn't wait for my answer. "Finish up, Dallas," she orders. "We've come to show you Muddy Springs's social life!"

Leila's got her dad's farm truck, and the three of us squish together on a seat lumpy from long use.

"Where to?" I ask.

"The tank."

It's just outside of town, not a man-made tank at all, but a wide, natural pool of water ringed by rock ledges. There's no one there when we arrive, but Julie Elise says, "Just wait."

"Is the water too deep for wading?" I ask, starting toward it, but I back off when Leila calls to be careful, there's snakes.

"So, Dallas," Leila asks, once we're stretched out and comfortable, "do you have a boyfriend?"

Julie Elise interrupts, "Listen!" She lifts her head for a better look down the road. "Isn't that Milton's car?"

Moments later he pulls in, and boys seem to erupt from the jalopy's doors. Julie Elise says, "I told you."

Then several more girls arrive, and after that the day kind of blurs into horseplay and pimiento-cheese sandwiches, iced tea, gossip, and flirting. And the boys do a little fishing, though they don't catch anything big enough to keep.

Julie Elise and Milton, who apparently were the hit of a high school talent night, occasionally launch into a hilarious routine about two fast-talking vaudeville stars, and I almost laugh myself silly listening to them.

It's midafternoon when Leila says, "Beatty, you never answered about whether you have a boyfriend."

"No one in particular," I say. "One of the things that's good about moving around is that you get to meet a lot of guys."

"That sounds a little wild," Julie Elise says, grinning at me.

But Leila persists, "Hasn't there been anyone you wanted to see more of?"

"Not yet. None I thought was that special."

I've been watching the fun around me, but now the scene

seems to shift a bit, moving over to make room for other scenes: Moss puzzling over that assortment of radio parts; trudging to town after a job; boosting Millie up on the airplane wing with us last evening.

I wonder if Moss really did give thought to helping out at the airfield. It would be good for him.

By the time Grif comes home for supper I've decided to bring it up myself. "He'd work just for some food, until he finds a real job," I explain. "And I'd help Clo with the extra cooking."

"Beatty," Grif says, "you don't have to sell me. Moss was raking the walk when I got there this morning, and he's been finding chores to do since."

Clo asks, "Then where is he? If he's working for food, he should be here to eat."

"He didn't want to intrude. I split my lunch with him, and when I go back I'll take him something more."

Feeling a bit thrown off balance—somehow I hadn't expected Moss to take things on himself so fast—I ask, "But… What about Millie? What did he do with her?"

"Said he left her at the caboose, feasting on grasshoppers. Clo, can we spare a bit extra for the dog, too? I wish we had a way to pay the boy real money."

9

$\mathcal{F}$RIDAY OF THE next week is my birthday. I find a
small, flat box on the breakfast table with a card saying,
"For a special girl as she turns fifteen." It's got everybody's
name on it, all my aunts' and Grif's and Dad's.

"Aren't you going to undo the tissue?" Clo asks, her eyes
shining.

I can't imagine… Carefully, I unwrap a lady's watch, a silver
rectangle of filigree around a face with hour and minute hands
so delicate they look like lace.

"Oh," I say, "it's beautiful. But how can I—I mean, how
can—" I stop, uncertain how to ask if, when times are so hard,
this hasn't cost more than should be spent on me.

Clo says, "And, Beatty, I'm supposed to tell you from everyone, 'Happy birthday.' Your father included, though he'll tell
you himself this evening."

"Oh, Clo…"

"He called from Dallas to say the afternoon flight won't have
an extra seat, so he's catching a bus over instead. He's planning
to stay for the weekend."

"Really? So he's done being mad?"

"I guess."

Mrs. Granger, the airport director's wife that Clo's been getting to know, comes by in late morning with a card and an embroidered handkerchief. "That's happy birthday from me and Mr. Granger," she says.

For lunch Leila and Julie Elise take me to the malt shop, where there's a lot of joking—the boys all want to know if I'm just Sweet Sixteen or if I'm Sweet Sixteen and Never Been Kissed?

"Fifteen," I tell them. "I'm exactly fifteen."

Milton says that wasn't the working part of the question.

And in the early afternoon, as I'm riding to the airport to see what's going on there, I meet Moss walking up the highway. "Hey," I call as we near each other, "where are you going?"

The tips of his ears reddening, Moss says, "I heard it was your birthday. I thought to take you these."

Then I realize what's he's carrying, a bouquet of wildflowers, stems wrapped in wet newspaper.

"Moss, where did you find them? They're lovely."

Before I think about what I'm doing, I give him a quick peck on his cheek. It's just like the ones I gave Clo and Grif over the watch, just a quick thank-you, but it startles us both as much as being touched by a hot cinder would have.

Quickly I step back. "They're lovely, Moss," I tell him again. "Thank you."

"You're welcome."

"I should go back to the cabin so I can put them in water," I say, and he nods, but neither of us actually moves. Not until

Millie comes bounding out of the field with a stick she wants us to throw.

For my birthday dinner, Clo makes a pot roast, along with new potatoes and peas. Also, she's traded some hand sewing for eggs from the chickens that the tourist court owners keep out back. Now the whites are in an angel food cake, the yolks baked into the sunshine yellow of ladyfinger layers.

"Which cake do you want candles on?" she asks.

"Both."

The table is already pretty with Moss's flowers arranged in a canning jar, and Clo's got me setting it with party napkins she's made from scraps of material. "Anything else I can do?" I ask.

"Just go watch for your father. He ought to be arriving any minute."

The words are hardly out of her mouth when Muddy Springs's only cab drives up. Dad pulls out his overnight grip and hands me postcards he's picked up in Memphis and Saint Louis, Shreveport, Atlanta.

"I should start a collection," I say. "Thanks."

Clo brings out a pitcher of ice water and tells us to visit while she finishes up inside.

As soon as Dad's settled in a lawn chair I say, "Dad, I was talking to the airport mechanic the other day—"

"Kenzie?" he asks. "How did you run into him?"

"—I just did. And he told me he used to fly some with my mother. Why didn't you ever tell me she was a pilot?"

The late-day sun is coming in sideways and strong against one side of Dad's face, and now its warm glare shows his jaw tightening. "No reason," he says.

"But she was one? That's true?"

Dad doesn't deny it, but he doesn't volunteer anything extra.

"Why won't you tell me about her?" I ask. "I know I've never asked much, but I didn't need to as long as I could picture her looking like anybody else's mother—sick, of course, and the picture was hazy, but it made sense. Only now I'm hearing she wasn't like other mothers. Flying…Dad, that's what you do…"

"Don't be foolish, Beatty," Dad snaps. "What she did wasn't the same at all."

I try to get him to explain, but Dad backs off, and when Grif's car pulls in the tourist court, Dad practically springs up to greet him.

"Happy birthday again!" Grif calls to me. "See who's with me?"

Moss looks as if his cleaning project the last couple of hours has been himself. His skin is shiny from scrubbing, and he's wearing what I'm pretty sure is an old pair of pants and a shirt of Grif's, now starched and ironed.

I see Clo noticing appreciatively, though she doesn't say anything.

"Beatty, introduce your friend," Dad tells me.

"Hello, sir," says Moss.

Clo's dinner is wonderful, though I feel sorry for Moss. Dad must think he's a boyfriend of mine who needs interrogating.

And, of course, Moss doesn't have good answers for things like "What's your father do, Moss?" and "How far along in school are you?"

Moss doesn't try to dodge the questions, though. "My pa's

an automobile mechanic," he says. "Only there weren't work at home all last year, so he went lookin' for it elsewhere."

"And you?" Dad asks.

"I guess I need work more 'n I need school."

For some reason—I suppose because of how Dad is examining Moss—I notice Moss's grammar more than I usually do, and I wish I could stop his mistakes.

When Clo asks, "Moss, a second piece of cake?" and he answers, "I'm obliged. I ain't had none like this ever," I cringe for him.

"Beatty?" Clo asks.

"Yes, please," I say. "I *haven't* had *any* like this in a long time, either."

Moss flushes, and I realize I've hurt instead of helped.

Still, when Dad asks where he's living, Moss begins, "I ain't—" Then he backs up to say, carefully, "I don't have any real home right now, but—"

Interrupting to keep him from mentioning that abandoned caboose, which I know would make Dad uneasy, I risk asking about the other thing that's been on my mind. "Dad, that woman who almost flew me down, Annie Boudreau? Where did you know her from?"

For a moment I think Dad's going to get angry again, but he doesn't. Instead he answers shortly, "She was one of your mother's cronies."

"Why would she care how I'm being raised?"

Clo says, "Beatty, it's natural if she was a friend of your mother's that—"

But Dad cuts her off. "It's not her business."

Embarrassed silence follows until Grif thinks to tell about that plane coming down in the farm field last week.

"Yeah? What kind?" Dad asks.

Moss says, "It was a Lockheed Vega, sir. Kenzie told me."

Dad laughs. "So you've met Kenzie, too! He put you to work? I've seen him do it even to a pilot."

I start to tell Dad that Kenzie's had me busy also, but Moss answers first. "Not put me to work, exactly," he says. "But we fixed an oil pump together. It was pretty new, but there was—were—a couple places—a couple *of* places where it was worn…"

Dad frowns. "Did Kenzie say what caused the wear?"

And then Moss is sketching something on a scrap of paper. "What we figured," he's telling my dad, "see, the worn places was—were—inside here, and—"

Dad asks, "But how did you go about fixing it? I'd have thought the whole thing would have to be replaced."

"Oh no, sir," Moss says. "We just overhauled—"

"Beatty," Clo says, getting up, "should we leave the guys to the mechanical talk?"

Moss and Grif leave in time for Grif to meet the 10:35 mail flight, but even after that Clo and Dad and I sit outside visiting. The two of them get going on stories from when they were kids. "Remember, Collin, that time you got sent to your room without supper and climbed out the window and down a grapevine, only to stumble on the cat and break your arm…"

"You can't remember, Clo. You weren't even born yet."

"But I've heard about it often enough from Maud and Fanny. And heard how, even while you were yowling in pain, you couldn't stop laughing about how surprised the cat was…"

It reminds me of what Clo told me about my dad when he was young, that he was a joyful noise.

I don't glimpse that side of him very often. And when I do, it's usually at a time like this, when everybody sits outside and retells old stories, waiting for a summer night to cool. I've heard the stories told the same way at Fanny's house, on the porches at Grandpa's and Maud's, on the lawn of the boardinghouse where Clo lived after Grandpa died and before she married Grif.

Tonight, though, I'm wondering what stories my mother would tell if she'd lived and could sit with us and add her own. What would be the memories she'd most cherish?

And, asking as the thought forms, I say, "Dad, there's another birthday present I'd like. Will you please take me for a plane ride? Just so I can know how it feels?"

Dad shakes his head, but Clo suddenly leans forward as though to challenge him. "Why not, Collin?" she asks. "Have you any reason not to let Beatty see what you find so special up there? How long are you going to cut your *daughter* off from your life?"

Dad grips the arms of his chair as though to restrain an angry answer, and I jump in to head off an argument.

"It's all right, Dad," I say. "I just thought maybe, since you seemed to consider letting me go with you that day your copilot suggested it…"

Grif, who's returned in time to hear this last, says, "There're open seats on tomorrow morning's eastbound flight, Collin. You two could have a quick lunch in Dallas and catch the westbound back."

Dad, looking cornered, finally gives a reluctant "OK."

THE SUN IS streaming in the windows when I wake up, coming in so strong I know right away it's at least mid-morning. I scramble out of a tangle of sheets. "Clo," I call, "what time is it? Where are you?"

"Here, Beatty," she says, opening the screen door.

"Why did you let me oversleep? Is Dad still in his cabin? We're going to miss our plane!"

"No, no. Take it easy, Beatty," Clo tells me. "You're going out this afternoon instead, taking the westbound flight as far as El Paso. Which means you'll get to eat dinner and stay in a hotel."

"Great! But why?"

"Because the pilot on the airmail milk run this morning got sick and your father offered to fill in on the next leg. He said he can connect with the afternoon flight, so all you have to do is meet him on board."

"Then I better pack a bag. Clo, don't you wish you were me?"

———

Bicycling to the airport, I can't resist stopping by Joe's Texas Auto Parts.

Joe eyes the little travel case that I've got wedged in my bike basket. "Some passenger forget that?" he asks.

"No."

"Doing another errand for your aunt?"

"No."

"I know. You're running away from home!"

"No! Joe, I'm going flying. In a plane!"

"Well, I guess, since I don't see no wings on you." He waves at the sky. "I'll be watchin'."

I detour by the hangar to tell Kenzie.

"Hey," I yell as I head inside, "did you hear? I'm going flying."

As my eyes adjust to the shadowed light, I make out three coveralled bodies huddled near the motor of the *Gold Lightning* plane. Something *pings* and someone says, "Dang, I thought we had it."

Then they turn, and I see they're Kenzie, Moss, and Annie Boudreau herself—all grease smeared and looking like their minds are still mostly on their work.

"Well? What'd you say?" Kenzie asks.

Feeling a little foolish, I repeat, "I just dropped by to tell you that Dad and I are going to take the afternoon plane to El Paso. So..." I try to joke but can't keep a tremor from my voice ". . . Lindsey Donnough's daughter is going to fly!"

"About time!" Kenzie says, and Gold Lightning, her voice sounding uneven, says, "She would have liked that."

———

"Grif?" I ask, "is Dad's plane going to be on time?"

He finishes marking changes on a weather map, working from a clipboard of hourly forecasts. Then, avoiding my eyes, he answers, "Beatty, the dispatcher in Lubbock says Collin took the mail flight on from there."

"But...he was coming back here to take me for a plane ride."

"I'm sorry, Beatty."

"Aren't there any other pilots in Texas? Couldn't somebody else have done the mail?"

Grif shifts uncomfortably, and his silence is all the answer I need. "Dad volunteered, didn't he?" I say. "Offered to work so he could get out of taking me up?"

"Beatty, there'll be other times..."

And more times when Dad will take off instead of doing something he doesn't want to do. Why does he think it's OK to just leave things he doesn't want to deal with?

I try to talk Grif into setting things up so I can make the trip by myself, but of course he says, "Beatty, you know I can't do that."

"But—"

"Listen," he says, pointing to a pile of bulging sacks out by the scale, "five hundred pounds of experimental seed just showed up marked to go on the Tri-Motor coming in, and I've got to refigure all my load allowances. I just can't take time to talk with you now."

Outside, I jam my travel case into my bike basket. I hope Dad is feeling so guilty that he is absolutely miserable!

Over by the hangar, the *Gold Lightning* plane rolls into view, pushed by Kenzie, Moss, and Annie.

Annie climbs in the rear of the cockpit, and Moss goes around front to hand-prop the plane.

"Contact," he calls, and she shouts back, "Contact."

Grasping the top of the propeller blade, Moss pulls it down and through, jumping back as the engine comes to life.

And then I watch, unbelieving, as Moss climbs in the plane's front seat. What's he doing?

I drop my bike and run toward them while the propeller rotates faster and the plane begins moving.

"Hey!" I call. "Moss! Annie! Wait!" but my words must be drowned out in the motor noise.

"Kenzie!" I shout. "What are they doing?"

"Just takin' a test ride," he shouts back. "Checking how our adjustments are."

"But why's Moss getting to go?"

" 'Cause Annie's dragging him along, making sure her mechanic's got faith in his work. And I guess to keep him from being too left out when you go off with your dad."

"But—"

Hot tears blur my view of the takeoff.

It is not fair, none of it.

Dad didn't have any business going back on his promise, and Grif…Grif's probably glad I won't be going: He'll have an easier time getting on all that seed.

I should be glad for Moss, really. I can't begrudge him.

But if Moss is going flying, then I am, too.

I go back to the terminal, where Grif is hurrying to get everything done for the flight Dad and I were supposed to be on. The plane is already making its final approach.

"I'll take these for you," I say, nodding toward two suitcases that are standing near the seed sacks.

He waves his appreciation and hurries past. He's carrying paperwork, manifests showing who and what's going on the plane here, and that they won't bring the weight total to more than the airplane can lift.

I pick up the luggage and call to the couple it belongs to that it's time to come out on the ramp. They follow, watching me set their things down on a freight cart. When I return to the terminal, I have the place to myself.

Quickly I drag three of the sacks of seed into the janitor's closet, hoping that together they come in somewhere near my own 113 pounds. There're enough bags left for loading that I hope Grif won't notice three missing.

Then I go outside to wait. As I watch the plane taxi in—another Tri-Motor, a blunt-lined ship of corrugated metal well nicknamed the *Tin Goose*—I have only one question. Can I get away with this?

The plane's three propellers have barely stopped when the activity that I'm counting on begins: Kenzie hurries up in his service truck; Grif wheels over a freight cart; the plane's door opens; and the copilot escorts off the few passengers, who want to stretch their legs. They seem to gulp fresh air.

Last out is the pilot. I see my chance when he and Grif take their clipboards of papers into the shade on the plane's far side.

Now! I think. *Go!*

My heart's pounding a mile a minute, even though I can still give an excuse if I have to: *Just looking,* I might say. *I came to straighten up.*

But there's nobody inside the plane, and I don't have to explain myself.

I take in the single leather seats lined up along the windows, their aluminum frames anchored to a steeply inclined linoleum floor. Seven seats on each side, fourteen altogether, the lines stretch forward toward the cockpit. Open shelves above hold a few small items, and at several places, window shades are pulled down against the afternoon sun.

Immediately to my left there's a bulkhead with a door that I open. It leads into a lavatory, clean but smelling like someone was sick in there not too long ago. The odor is enough to bring on doubts, but before I can reconsider, I hear the bumps and thumps of cargo being loaded in a wing bin and voices approaching the passenger door. Quickly I slip into the lavatory, pull the door shut, and crouch low so I won't be seen through the small porthole windows on either side.

My plan is to wait until we're in the air before I move into the passenger cabin. Then I'm going to try to slip into one of the rear seats. I doubt the other passengers will notice.

Or maybe I'm hoping, more than planning…

One part of me cannot believe I am doing this, stowing away, taking off without any idea how I'm going to return. It's the part that says I better back out now while I can.

And the other part cuts a deal. *Maybe I'll get off if I can without anybody noticing. But if I don't get the chance… Then I'm on my way!*

A man's voice calling, "Let's board," decides it.

For the next several minutes everything comes to me as sound. I listen to the muffled noise of people settling into their seats, and I hear clangs and knocks coming from outside the plane's thin, hot metal skin. I identify a dragging noise as Kenzie taking down the fuel hose.

There are more voices—pilot and copilot?—someone asking, "Finished your flight checks?" and then, unmistakably, the *clunk* of the door being shut.

"Welcome to you new folks," I hear a man say, the copilot, I suppose. "Everyone ready to go? Seat belts fastened? I'm afraid strong winds are going to give us more turbulence."

To my right an engine turns over and settles into a plane-vibrating roar. Another off to my left rumbles on. Then the one on the nose. The plane begins to roll forward, and suddenly I'm really scared at what I'm doing. I want to yell that the plane has to be stopped, but I can't seem to get any words out.

I feel us going faster and faster, bumping over rough ground, and I reach around for something to grab on to. And then—just when I'm expecting…what? How will it feel to go up?—the plane stops.

For a moment I'm sure it's because I've been discovered and someone's going to jerk open the door, yank me up, and shout, *Stowaway!*

But instead the motors thunder a hundred times louder, revving up as if they're being tested, and then we're rolling again.

Cautiously I stand to look out. The airfield seems to be rushing past, its uneven surface a blur. Faster and faster we go, the speed pushing me backward, and I reach for something to brace myself against. Faster…until we're almost skimming the ground, hitting the ridges of the uneven earth… faster…

A bad jolt throws me off balance, and though I grab at the sink and door handle to catch myself, I'm thrown to the floor. Then, as I huddle half wedged between the toilet and the wall, I feel the plane angle up. The bumping stops. I realize…we're in the air!

An instant later the floor tilts sideways under me, and I hear someone call above the plane's noise, "Look! You can see the reservoir."

I pull myself to my feet but get only the barest glimpse out before a sudden drop throws me off balance again. The lavatory door cracks open—I must have unlatched it when I fell—and I hear someone groan, "Oooooh."

I reach out to pull the door closed, but another dip in our flight makes it swing wider open. A smell I only half noticed before—oil and exhaust and maybe old body sweat—seems to hover and then settle in a cloud around my head.

Now the plane hits that turbulence the copilot mentioned and commences really bouncing. Buffeted side to side, it bucks in sudden drops and rises.

"Talk about air pockets," someone says.

"Be glad we're not sitting in the rear," a man answers. "When it's rough here under the wings, the tail's worse."

We drop again, and this time my stomach goes halfway to my throat.

Someone calls, "Anybody got an airsick cup?"

Oh no! Why did he have to make me think about that?

The next several minutes—they seem like hours—are agony. The oil stink smothers me, the hot air is suffocating, my stomach is churning around and around.…Please…I can't let myself throw up. I can't. I can't.…

"Where's those airsick cups?" a voice shouts, and through the swinging lavatory door I see a man lurching toward me.

The copilot puts me in a backseat. He orders, "You just stay here, Miss Donnough," in a voice so cold and hard I'm afraid to even raise the window shade.

A few minutes later I feel the plane tilt to one side as we circle around, and I understand I am not going to El Paso or anywhere else special today. I'm only going back where I started from.

Chapter

11

THE TRI-MOTOR TOUCHES down just long enough to drop me off—and I get the distinct impression the captain would have dropped me from a window if he'd thought he could have gotten away with it. As it is, he doesn't cut the Tri-Motor's engines when he stops on the airport ramp, and they throw a fine spray of oil over me as I scramble out.

I expect Grif to be furious, but when I see how drawn his face is I realize he is too worried for anger.

"I'm really sorry, Grif. I was so disappointed about my ride with Dad, and—"

"Not now," he interrupts. "I've got to do something with that seed you hid and then try to straighten out the rest of this mess."

And Kenzie, in the hangar, is blunt. "Don't you know your stunt could cost Grif his job?" he says.

"*He* didn't stow away. I did."

"But he's responsible both for this place and for you."

Moss, looking like he'd rather be anywhere but in here over-hearing, ducks closer to what he's working on.

"Beatty," Clo says when I go back to our tourist cabin, "how could you?"

"I guess Grif called?"

"Mrs. Granger came by just to tell me." Tears well in my aunt's eyes. "Don't you know the trouble you've made?"

I try to tell her how I wish I could undo this whole after-noon, but she hurries through to the bedroom.

"Clo," I say, following. "I'm really sorry."

She goes around me and outside, no more ready than Grif to hear my apologies.

I learn what happens by eavesdropping. Or maybe that's not the right word, because I don't have to sneak and hide to listen, just take in what's being said around me.

I'm just grateful it doesn't include talk of involving Dad.

And Grif doesn't lose his job—I think because Mrs. Granger gets Mr. Granger to put in a placating word with Grif's division manager. But he is placed on probation, and he tells Clo, "Another slip and I'm out."

There's an unspoken understanding that I won't go any-where near the airport, and in the next days I don't much know what to do with myself instead.

Clo and I pick out material and a pattern for lightweight dresses, but there's quiet between us as we lay out tissue, and pin and cut.

The girls come for me a couple of times, but I can't seem to enjoy myself much with them.

And when Moss appears at the door it's clear he's still bewildered by what I did—and maybe embarrassed for me, which is much worse.

"Millie doing OK?" I ask.

"Yeah."

"And you're still helping Grif?"

"Some, but Kenzie more. He got paid a tip the other day for a job we worked on together, and he gave me most of it. I sent half to Ma and bought me some food with the rest so I won't be so beholden to you all."

"I'm proud of you, Moss," I tell him, no idea how to get into the web of things I want to ask about, tell about, explain.

"Beatty," he says, his ears reddening the way they did when he brought me birthday flowers, "I miss seein' you at the airport."

"Yes…well…I guess I won't be going back."

I do wish I could undo things. I'd almost be willing to take a vow never to go up in a plane, if that would unwind the trouble I've caused.

I realize how precarious I've made things when Clo's sewing machine gets lowered into its case to clear space for a rented typewriter. Her eyes steady on a propped-up lesson book, she taps, *jjjj ffff jjjj ffff…bed red fed jut…*

She's thinking she might have to go back to work and might need to earn more than she did as a file clerk.

Just watching her makes me angry, and, of course, I don't have anyone to be angry at except myself. Unless maybe it's Dad, who would have prevented me doing something so *stupid* if he'd just kept his promise.

Along with the regret and guilt, though, what surprises me

72

is the loss I feel, the tug that gnaws whenever I hear an airplane engine overhead.

It's as though my days are marked off by the planes that fly regularly into Muddy Springs: the 6:00 A.M. milk run, then the morning passenger flight heading east, and the afternoon one westbound. I go to sleep listening to the night mail plane come in.

With each engine sound I imagine what might be going on at the airport. I picture Grif working the desk, Moss washing the service truck, and Kenzie tinkering at his workbench. I hear the radio squeal and see the landing lights come on.

It makes no sense to care so much for a place I hardly know, but every time I think of it, I feel hollow.

I tell myself I should keep busy, move along the way I always have. Visit the malt shop. Grab a ride to the tank.

Or call Aunt Fanny and ask if she'll let me share her boardinghouse room until her own house is ready. I could sleep on the floor.

And I do actually get as far as the telephone in the tourist court office.

"Operator," I say, stretching on tiptoe to talk into the mouthpiece, "I'd like to place a long-distance call to Dallas." I give her the number of the insurance office where Fanny's got a temporary job. "And please let me know the charges."

It rings, and then Fanny herself answers, surprised to be hearing from me.

"Beatty, is something wrong?"

"I…yes…," I begin. And then I can't go further. "No, Aunt Fanny. I just was going to write a thank-you note for my birthday watch and decided to call instead."

"It's an expensive way to say thank you, Beatty. But you're welcome."

I replace the receiver carefully and count out my pocket money while waiting for the operator to ring back with what I owe.

Dad finds out what I did when he gets his June 30 paycheck and sees he's been docked the cost of the fuel it took to return me to Muddy Springs. The next day he deadheads down from New York—comes all this way as a nonrevenue passenger on another pilot's flight—just to talk to me face-to-face.

"You were a fool, Beatty," he says, "taking a risk like you did, causing a plane to divert from its flight plan. Didn't you think how your actions might be dangerous to you and everyone on the plane?"

Dad gets more upset as he talks, his face becoming ruddy and his eyes glistening with held-in anger. "Flying's not some sport that always turns out right.

"And look what you did to Grif. He's got a hard-enough job being everything from radioman to dispatcher to ticket agent without you bringing his boss down on him."

Grif raises and drops his hands as though to say maybe things aren't quite as bad as Dad's making them out.

"Dad," I say, "Grif knows I'm sorry."

"Get your things packed, Beatty. I'm going to call Fanny and Maud and see if they can't work something out between them."

"You want me to leave Muddy Springs? Dad, I don't want to go."

But he's already walking to the tourist court office.

"Dad, wait...Grif...Clo?"

I grope for ideas, only coming up with a single, sorry one I realize isn't likely to be accepted—but I offer it anyway.

"Grif, Moss says he's not helping you so much now that Kenzie has him doing mechanic stuff. If I promise to do only what you tell me, will you let me take his place? I'll do any kind of work...I'd like to make up for the trouble I've caused you."

Poor Grif: I can hear how it pains him to answer, "Beatty, I'm sorry."

I go to bed listening to the murmurs of Grif and Clo, murmurs still going on when I wake up in the middle of the night.

Of course, I was asking way too much.

Early the next morning, though, it's Grif who calls, "Some fried eggs, Beatty?"

"Where's Clo?" I ask.

"I let her sleep."

I'm squeezing us orange juice when he says, "About your idea. You've got to understand how important this airline job is to your aunt and me. If anything else goes wrong, whether it's my fault or not..."

"It's OK, Grif," I tell him. "I do understand."

"So, if I let you help out—which I can't unless my division manager at the airline says so—then..."

"But I thought..." *Is he saying what I think he is?* "Grif, you're considering it? You'd take that chance for me?"

"No, Beatty," he answers, "probably not. But I would for Clo, and it's what she's asked."

Later on I try to thank my aunt, but it's so hard I wind up offering a joke. "Clo, are you forgetting that the easy part of taking care of me is being able to send me on?"

She says, "It's easy only as long as you want to go."

Dad washes his hands of the whole decision.

"I told you only fools take unneeded risks, and here you're taking one with Grif's job. But I guess you're your mother's daughter."

"What do you mean by that?"

Clo steps between me and him, the quick temper she never shows for herself now flaring up. "And Beatty's also *your* daughter, Collin. Though staying on to fix what she's responsible for—that's not a trait she gets from you."

For a moment Dad stares stony faced at his sister, his anger apparent. Then his features suddenly relax. "I've got a flight to catch."

12

THE FOLLOWING WEDNESDAY, I ride to work with Grif. "Was it hard to get permission for me to do this?" I ask.

"I didn't exactly get it," Grif answers. "My division manager just agreed not to notice, as long as nothing happens he can't ignore. He said he has seven kids himself and every one of them's needed something sometime."

Oh.

"So," I ask, "what do I do first?"

"Golly, Beatty, I don't know. Usually Moss or I put up the flag and rake the walkway. Why don't you start with that?"

And then I clean out the flower bed and scour the grounds for trash and wash the outsides of the terminal windows. Moss tries to help, but I don't let him. "Doesn't Kenzie have something you can do?" I ask.

"Yes, but it ain't right, Beatty, you doin' this work."

"Moss," I tease, "are you worried I'm taking your job?"

"No." Moss sounds troubled. "But you're not...Your people ain't...This ain't ladies' work."

"You told me you never knew a girl to do shop work, either. Just what do the girls of your acquaintance do?"

He sees I'm kidding him, but he's still flustered. "I don't know, Beatty. But they weren't never none of 'em like you."

"And ain't none of the boys I ever knew like you, either."

"You're making fun of me."

"Yeah. Do you mind?"

"No."

"Now what?" I ask Grif.

"I don't know...Here..." He hands me a notebook full of company bulletins. "Some of those cover the duties of ground personnel," he says. "Why don't you read though them and figure out for yourself what you can help with?"

I take the binder outside, where I find a nice shady patch of grass by the side of the terminal, get comfortable, and look to see what Grif's given me.

The bulletins don't seem to be arranged in any order, but paging through them I begin to glimpse the huge number of things an airline has to be concerned about.

I skim safety regulations regarding clearances of passenger flights, seeing things as shapeless as the weather defined in measured phrases: "visibility less than...less than one thousand feet of ceiling..."

Flipping to the beginning of the notebook, I find instructions for providing courteous, efficient service. The second part of that memo is missing, though, and in its place are directions for preparing load manifests. After that comes a bulletin amending the clearance regulations I read about earlier.

Dang...I smush a tiny red bug moving up my leg. *Well, at least I know my next project.*

And finding Grif, I say, "How about if I put this operations manual in order? It seems pretty disorganized."

"Would you?" he asks, and the real appreciation in his voice makes me feel wonderful.

At lunchtime I go hunting for Moss but hang back when I see him at the workbench with a couple of men I don't know. Moss is busy filing on a metal part, nodding along while the two men visit.

Kenzie, coming by, says, "They're just crop dusters killing time with 'hangar flying.' Go on over."

I shake my head, suddenly shy.

"Suit yourself."

I eat my sandwich sitting on the concrete ramp area, leaning back against the terminal building. All but the last bite, anyway. Millie snatches that away.

"You know," I tell her, "a really well-trained dog wouldn't steal food. And where'd you appear from?"

She offers a length of belly for me to rub.

"Aren't you supposed to stay at the caboose when Moss is down here?"

She jabs me with a foot.

"OK, OK!"

But something on the landing field diverts her attention, and she races away. After flushing a bird that flies off, she chases it until she's almost out of sight.

Moss, joining me, laughs. "That crazy dog's gonna wear herself out. How come you ate without me? Kenzie said you come to the hangar and then left without saying nothing."

"*Anything*."

" 'Anything.' Beatty, you should of listened to those pilots. They was telling a story—"

"*Were* telling."

"Yeah. They *were* telling a story about this flight they was on—were on—when their engine conked and—"

"Moss, I'm sorry. I shouldn't keep correcting your grammar."

"I'm grateful." He looks at me kind of sideways. "I admire people not too proud to learn."

A man's voice behind us interrupts. "Are you Moss and Beatty?"

He's a cheerful-faced man, perspiring, in a straw hat and a business shirt and a tie. He says, "Thought I'd meet all this new help I've been hearing about. I'm Mr. Granger, by the way, and—"

He breaks off to exclaim, "Gol *darn* it! Look at those danged sheep. If I have told the ranchers around here once I have told them a thousand times, 'Keep your animals off the landing field. They are a hazard.' "

Millie has also spotted the band of ewes and lambs wandering onto the weedy hard-pack, and now she's running at them, a low-streaking blur of black and white. The confused animals dart this way and that, but Millie barks orders and nips at hooves until she's herded them off the field. Then she drops into a watchful crouch, appearing ready to defend the whole airport if they return.

"Well, gol *darn* it!" Mr. Granger repeats. "Ordinarily I don't want dogs on my airfield any more than I want sheep, but maybe I should hire that one."

Which, of course, he doesn't mean, but he doesn't chase her away, either.

"Well," I say to Moss after Mr. Granger's left, "it looks like you, Millie, and I all have jobs now."

"And not a one of us gettin' paid regular," he says.

I ask, "Do you mind?"

"Nope. Not so long as Kenzie and me keep gettin' enough tips so I can buy food and not take so much from you all. You?"

"I'm just glad to be here. And it's *Kenzie and I*."

"That's what I said."

"Beatty," Grif asks, "do you know how to work a type-writer?"

"Just what Clo's shown me."

What he needs typed up is an item for the company news-letter, a publication that the airline wants each station to con-tribute to.

"Grif, do you really think anybody cares that the Muddy Springs Airport shipped a wedding cake and was visited by a senator's wife last month?"

"Hey, you come up with something better."

Clo's waiting when Grif and I drive up at suppertime, her eyes anxious. "Everything went all right? No problems?"

"Best day since we got to Muddy Springs," Grif tells her. "Beatty was a real help."

"Oh, good," Clo says, pleasure flooding her face. "I want to hear all about it."

"Can I tell you later?" I ask. "Do I have time for a nap before we eat?"

Chapter

13

WHEN SATURDAY ROLLS around, Julie Elise and Leila and I go in town to the picture show. Afterward, while we're having sodas at the candy shop next door, the girls ask why I've been at the airfield so much.

"I'm working there," I answer, expecting them to be surprised, but they're not particularly. More envious, is like, until I mention it's a volunteer position. I immediately wish I'd kept quiet about that part, because I don't want to explain about the dumb thing I did stowing away.

"You're working for free?" Leila asks.

Julie Elise saves me answering by interrupting with her own suggestion. "Beatty, does this have something to do with that boy who's working out there?" She turns to Leila. "I met him when he came in my dad's place to look at a book on radios. He's adorable."

"That's not the reason," I protest, annoyed at her for thinking that, and also at myself for the blush I feel coloring my cheeks. "I'm working at the airport because I'm really needed. And Moss is just…"

"What, Dallas?" teases Julie Elise. "Just a country boy? No big-city polish?"

Leila says, "Country boys are the best kind."

Monday morning I'm up before Grif and Clo, actually impatient to get back at my job.

And I don't even mind too much when a whole family meeting someone on the eastbound flight seems bent on testing that "courteous and efficient service."

"Yes, ma'am," I tell the lady. "I'll be glad to watch your children for a bit."

"No, sir," I answer her husband, "finding you a newspaper won't be a bother at all."

And I do not once say aloud what I'm thinking: *Hey, kids! Use the door handle. I'm the one who cleans that glass panel you're pushing on!*

I'm glad, though, when they leave after watching the flight depart on schedule at 9:45 and Grif says, "Go on and take a break, Beatty."

I wander out to the hangar, where I find Kenzie visiting with Annie Boudreau and a man I don't recognize. Swapping stories, I suppose, since nearby them Moss is sweeping the floor so slow he must be listening in.

I start to leave, but then, instead, grab a dustpan and go to help.

Annie sees me and nods as she continues with what she's telling the other person, who turns out to be a government weatherman.

"Talk about missing calls!" she says. "You all were saying, 'Clear, visibility unlimited,' when anybody looking out a window could see fog so thick the birds were walking."

"Now," the man says, "if we got it right all the time, you'd complain we were taking the sport out of flying."

Annie waves a hand toward me. "Not so long as we have girls like this one to keep us on our toes. Did you hear about the scare she gave me, competing with my airplane for landing space?"

Of course, she tells the whole story about almost running me down, but she doesn't sound angry and, in fact, kind of includes me in the audience. Her next tale is a drawn-out one that's not showing any signs of ending when I look at my watch and see I'm due back at the terminal.

Moss hands me the broom. "I'll go," he says, "and you finish here."

"You don't mind?"

"Nah. I'd as soon help out one place as the other."

Annie, taking in the exchange, says, "But come closer, Beatty, so I can stop shouting."

And Kenzie adds, "Only don't stop sweeping. Moss ain't got under that workbench in a week."

The switch-about, me to the hangar and Moss to the terminal, soon becomes a regular part of the day. Not that we don't stick mostly to our given jobs: There's no way I can take Moss's place as a grease monkey, and Grif likes me behind the desk at check-in times, when he's busiest.

And I do enjoy being able to give a good answer when some passenger calls me "miss" and asks about a schedule or services in the air.

There's one really scary day when the airline division manager shows up unannounced. "Not an official inspection," he tells Grif. "Just thought I'd see how things are going. Where's this niece of yours?"

"This is Beatty," Grif tells him as I come over.

I see the man appraising me, and I think a silent *Thank you* I'm in a neat skirt and blouse, an outfit that might belong in an office. He nods, approvingly I hope, but all he says is, "Don't let your uncle down, young lady. He's gone to bat for you."

Later on, when he's leaving, he seeks me out. "I told Grif it's a rare station where I find an operations manual completely caught up. He says this one is your doing."

I nod.

"You reading some of it?"

"Yes, sir."

"Good."

Good... That's how I'm feeling about myself, about Muddy Springs, too, more and more.

Though I must admit that the things making me happy are the most unlikely assortment, like pieces of a dream and pieces of what's true, too overlapped for me to know which is which.

Dad—again done being angry, I guess, or maybe just deciding to ignore the fact we ever disagreed—has taken to sending me postcards of the places where he flies to. They're mostly black-and-white but sometimes tinted photographs of a city's downtown or a boulevard of palm trees and large houses. On the back he writes, "Be good," or "Help your aunt," or, on a picture taken from an airplane, "For your collection."

I suppose it's as close to flying as I'm likely to get any year soon. If anything, the more I become part of all that goes on at the airport, the more I realize how unlikely it is I'll get up in a plane myself.

Clo and I pick out a scrapbook to keep the postcards in, and

I fall asleep over it one evening while I'm trying to decide on the arrangement and where to put in a couple of cards from school friends.

Dreaming, I get myself somehow mixed up with the tree that blew down on Aunt Fanny's house, only instead of falling I get picked up by the wind and whirled off. I see, twirling under me, the Alamo and the new zoo in San Antonio's Brackenridge Park, the Baylor campus in Waco, a Dallas streetcar, and the city's downtown.

Faster and faster I circle, until suddenly I'm flung straight out, swept over miles of mostly empty land, and dropped smack down on the Muddy Springs airfield's regulation embedded identifying circle.

"Beatty," Clo says, shaking my arm. "You better put this work away and go to bed."

The next day Moss seems quieter than usual when we eat our lunch, and finally I ask, "Is anything wrong?"

"No," he answers. "I'm just thinkin'."

"About what?" I keep at the question until he pulls a postal card from his shirt pocket.

It's addressed to Moss Trawnley, General Delivery, Muddy Springs, Texas. The elaborate script is uneven, as though its flourishes and curlicues were formed painfully, one by one.

"From Ma," Moss tells me.

The back reads, "Dear Son, I hope you are well and get this. We are alright. We miss you but its best you stay on if you are working as there's still none extra here. Your brother walked for the first last week."

"You miss home?" I ask.

He nods. "Some. Beatty, I hate it I wasn't there to see the littlest take a step."

Now it's my own words that are painful, a question catching in my chest as I try to get it out as lightly as I can. "Are you thinking you'll go back?"

"I reckon not," Moss answers. "You see what Ma says."

I am sorry for him, though I'm also glad in a way.

I'm still hearing the wistfulness in his voice when a woman waiting for the westbound plane to be refueled takes a small corsage of rosebuds from her suit jacket and hands it to me. "Would you like these?" she asks. "They won't last the trip."

I put them in a jar of water, and when I get a chance I take it over to the hangar. Kenzie, out on the ramp working under the hood of his truck, sees them and calls, "Beatty, don't you be turning my hangar into any ladies' parlor."

"I'm not."

Moss is at the workbench, and I set the flowers down in front of him. He asks, "What's this?"

"Just something pretty for you to look at. You seemed kind of sad before, and I thought..." My voice trails off as I realize how silly it is for me to be giving flowers to a fellow, especially here, especially to this boy who needs just about everything in the world more than he needs roses.

But he thanks me. And then, like we're both remembering that moment when it was me thanking him for wildflowers, Moss bends his head to kiss me, a peck on my cheek that turns into a light touch on my lips.

"Dad blast it!" Kenzie's voice carries from the hangar doorway. "Will somebody tell this animal to untwine herself from my ankles?"

Moss quickly steps back, and I look around, seeing Kenzie and Millie silhouetted against bright light. Hoping Kenzie didn't see us clearly—hoping he spoke before his eyes could adjust to the dim shadows in here—I call, "Mill, why are you bothering people?"

Thunder rumbles in the distance, and the dog streaks from Kenzie's legs to mine.

"Are you afraid, girl?" I ask. "Don't worry. I promise I won't let any old storm come near you."

Kenzie asks, "And just how, Beatty Donnough, are you going to keep storms away? Face 'em off?"

"Maybe," I answer, "if I have to."

The thunder rumbles again, and Millie jumps from my ankles to Moss's arms, her tail knocking the jar of roses into Kenzie's pipe tobacco.

"Dad blast it," Kenzie says again. "Dogs and flowers… in my hangar…"

14

THE STORM NEVER does get any closer, but it sets up a whole string of windy days. Deplaning passengers look a kind of greenish pale, the wind sock stands straight out, and one of the field floodlights is blown down. Put back in place, the light works but burns out bulbs about as fast as they're put in.

Mr. Granger comes out to the airport to consult with Grif about it, and I tag along when they walk out to see what needs doing. Millie stays close to Mr. Granger's heels, eager for the bit of meat or cheese he's taken to bringing her.

"I think there's damage up the whole line, which already wasn't working too well," Grif says. "I've jury-rigged a fix as best I can, but probably we should get someone in to look at it."

"I hate to spend the money," Mr. Granger answers. "Revenue's low enough anyway, and we need to be putting it to new things like runways."

"It would be nice to pave at least that carved-out path that most planes take," Grif agrees. "One thing pilots and passengers do hate is having to push a plane that's stuck in mud." He pulls a screwdriver from his pocket and unfastens the light cover. "But nobody likes to fly into an airport without reliable field lights, either."

"I guess you're right," Mr. Granger says, shaking his head. "When I get a chance, I'll put a call in to the company we bought them from."

One day the wind gets so strong that the afternoon flight bypasses Muddy Springs altogether. With no work to do in the terminal, I help out in the hangar, where Mr. Granger's got Kenzie and Moss counting inventory.

"Quarter-inch rivets?" I ask, reading down a list, and Kenzie answers, "Forty-seven."

"Fifteen here," Mr. Granger says.

"Three-eighths inch?"

"I got 'em," Moss says. "Eighteen, nineteen...twenty-two in all."

Grif comes searching for something to eat. "Are there any of Clo's oatmeal cookies left?" he asks me.

"Sorry. Are you really hungry?"

"Not enough to worry about. Air over a plane's wings."

After he leaves I ask the others, "What does he mean by that?"

Kenzie chuckles. "I'd guess he means it's nothing, or not enough to worry about, anyway."

I'm still puzzled.

"Because," Kenzie says, "in one way, *nothing* is what air being rushed over the curved front of a plane's wing results in. It makes a space of almost nothing—a low-pressure area—over the slanted-down back side of the wing."

"Seems a roundabout way of talking," Moss says.

I look at a Travel Air biplane in for maintenance and see that, sure enough, the leading edges of its wings are rounded and the trailing edges tapered and narrow.

"So what's the point?" I ask. "I mean about low pressure over an airplane's wings?"

"So?!!" Kenzie practically sputters. "Why, it's that low pressure that gives a plane its lift, girl—that lets it leave the ground. Higher-pressure air underneath pushes up on the wing and lifts the whole airplane with it."

It's a difficult thing to grasp, but Kenzie tells me, "See for yourself. Blow your breath atop that piece of paper you're working on."

Holding one short edge curved over my fingers, I breathe across it.

"Harder!"

I blow my breath out evenly and with all the force I can, and watch the paper rise almost horizontal.

"See?" Kenzie says. "They're the same thing, what you just did breathing and the lift a plane gets when air rushes over its wings."

"A wonder," Moss says, getting paper to try it himself.

"More like a miracle," I say, looking from the tissue-thin inventory form in my hands to an airplane that must weigh close to a ton.

But I also wonder, *Is a plane leaving the ground more or less of a miracle when I understand how it works?*

Kenzie says, "Knowing the *why* of a thing makes it part yours."

Mr. Granger watches Moss for a moment before saying,

"Oh, what the heck." Then he reaches for his own piece of paper.

There's one place, though, where I'll probably never understand the *why* of things, and that's in the operations room.

The equipment there baffles me, and even if it didn't I'd probably stay out. The place isn't big enough for three people, and more and more often Moss and Grif are in there talking radios.

They began the day Moss brought Grif those tubes and parts from the caboose.

Grif told him, "I don't think you can make much of all this. You're missing some main items." But then he added, "Come on. We'll take the case off the station receiver so you can see what I mean."

Since that day, Moss has taken to finding excuses to be in the terminal when he knows Grif's likely to be talking to an incoming plane or collecting weather information from a couple of ham operators who radio rather than call it in. He watches intently when Grif struggles with dials and knobs to make broken transmissions come in clearer.

And in quiet moments Moss studies the radio manual he bought from Julie Elise's dad—a purchase I suspect he made instead of food, though he's too proud to say. Right off, he memorized the page showing the Morse code, and sometimes I see him tapping out a message on a tabletop.

"What's that?" I ask when he practices over and over, *DAH–DAH, di–di–dit.*

"*M S,* for Muddy Springs," he answers.

"Why do you need to learn that? Morse code?"

" 'Cause it takes less radio power than talking does. Also, it reaches farther."

Another day I find Moss frowning over the manual's tightly printed words regarding voice transmission. I suspect half of them are words Moss has never heard, much less read. "You need help with that?" I ask.

But he says, "No. I'm figurin' it out. Ain't—isn't—it amazing how this all works? That radio can send whatever you say out through the air, all the way up to planes…" Moss pauses. "It's not like there's wires connecting you."

"It *is* pretty wonderful," I say.

"Like a miracle," Moss answers. "A sheer and outright miracle."

About this time, I make a discovery of my own—just what it was that made Millie one of Colonel Bo Marshall's Stars of the Silver Screen. Or, rather, Mr. Granger and I make it together.

It's another windy day, and Mr. Granger's come out to talk some more about those field-light repairs, as well as to check on other matters, like that we're not wasting supplies or using electricity unnecessarily.

"Revenue," he says sternly, "got to conserve the revenue."

But then he has me get a soup bone that he "just happened to notice" was in his car. "Come on," he tells me, "let's go see if Millie's earning her keep."

She's not.

Instead she's chasing things from a blown-over trash can, playing all by herself with scattering torn lunch boxes and papers. She snatches a piece of cardboard from midair, only to drop it and tear after a cup that's spinning across the ground.

"Would you look at that dog go!" Mr. Granger says. The next thing I know he's making a paper airplane. He throws it high and calls, "Fetch, Millie," as the wind sails it aloft.

Millie takes off, speeding twenty-five feet, fifty, racing to catch up. Then, just as the paper plane nose-dives, she leaps high and grabs it, flipping over in a twisting somersault. And she actually lands on her feet.

"Wow!" I say, and Mr. Granger and I clap. "Good *girl*!"

Millie prances to us and bows, her front legs flat on the ground and her rear up. She nods her head right and left.

"That dog's as good as the trained ones I saw at an air show a while ago," Mr. Granger says. "Better, maybe."

"I'd like to see an air show sometime," I tell him. "But how do dogs fit in?"

"Just crowd pleasers to keep things going between events." He laughs at Millie, who can't decide whether to eat the bone or bury it. "But the dogs alone were worth my fifty-cent ticket."

"I bet when Millie was in Hollywood she earned more than fifty cents," I tell him.

"And there she didn't have an airfield to patrol," Mr. Granger agrees.

The other thing that happens about this time is that I return from a Saturday afternoon with Julie Elise and Leila to find Clo sitting at her typewriter but reading a letter from Aunt Maud. It begins, "Fanny and I've got the Beatty Rotation reworked. See if it suits."

The schedule they're planning calls for me to start school

this fall in Waco, do spring semester in Dallas with Fanny, whose house ought to be fixed by then, and return to Clo, wherever she is, next summer.

"Sound good to you, Beatty?" Clo asks, but her voice is strangely flat.

"Not really," I answer. I pause, realizing this may be the first time I've ever objected to the aunts' arrangements for me. "I'd rather stay with you. And…I guess…stay here in Muddy Springs."

"But you know that once the regular station manager comes back here we'll move on."

"Mrs. Granger said maybe he won't return at all."

"The airline still might put another, more senior man in his place. The most likely thing, Beatty, is that Grif will have to go back to shifting from station to station every week or two."

"Kind of a Grif Rotation," I say.

Joking's as good an answer as any, I guess, since there's no point in belaboring what Clo and I both understand: The plan Fanny and Maud have proposed makes sense, and there's no good alternative to offer.

The idea of seeing an air show stays on my mind, partly, I suppose, because I'm glad for any thought that keeps me from remembering that I'll be leaving Muddy Springs in another month. Going without ever having had a real ride in an airplane.

What else, though, keeps me thinking about air shows is some of the hangar stories I hear about my mother.

Kenzie has taken to occasionally introducing me to visiting pilots—the older ones—by saying, "You recall Lindsey Donnough? This here's her daughter."

And then I might hear a tale about some adventure my pilot-mother had: how she taught some flying instructors a thing or two; how she once rescued an injured miner by taking her Jenny into a mountain meadow so narrow no other pilot would consider it; how she liked to test the limits of canvas and wire and wood.

Or I might hear of air exhibitions she took part in, in her own plane or in whatever more powerful one she could borrow. One man tells about seeing my mother fly a complete loop and come out of it so low down she flew *under* an electric line.

All that afternoon I turn over in my mind a picture of her thrilling crowds as she performed in the sky.

"She was a stunt flyer!" I tell Moss. "Can you imagine?"

"Hardly," he says. "Leastways, I can't imagine my ma doing that stuff."

There's a sad, resigned note in his voice, enough to make me ask, "Did you hear from your mother again?"

Moss nods. "She says Pa wrote that he's hoping to sign on for government relief work out West. She says meantime I should send home a bit more."

I put down a flash of anger at this woman who just wants to *take* from Moss. That's how it seems to me, anyway.

Maybe, though, she doesn't know he's still working just for tips and that what money he does send home is more than most would spare. I've seen him at the grocery story buying cornmeal, dried beans, wilted greens from the day-old bin. Other than for that radio manual he probably hasn't spent one unnecessary penny on himself.

It's easier to be angry at his mother than to think about him going elsewhere to find work.

"What you need, Moss," I tell him, "is to get the airport to pay you a regular salary."

"Kenzie says so, too," Moss answers. "But Mr. Granger says that much as he'd like to, himself, he'd never get the airport board to agree. Not enough revenue."

Later on that afternoon, I take a Dr. Pepper out back of the terminal building. Millie sees me and comes running in from the airfield.

"This isn't for you, girl," I tell her. "But you can sit down and listen while I tell you all that's wrong with the world. Money, for one thing. Or needing more than you have."

Millie licks the wet outside of the soda bottle.

"Yuck, Mill," I say, wiping if off with my skirt. "Didn't Colonel Bo Marshall teach you any manners? Or did you make so much money for him that he let you get away with whatever you wanted?"

And then, an instant later, I'm hurrying inside, calling, "Grif, when's Mr. Granger coming out here again?"

"I'M HERE NOW," Mr. Granger answers from the wall phone behind the counter. He's holding the telephone receiver. "What—" Then he breaks off to listen. "I see. Well, whenever you can, anyway."

Hanging up, he grumbles, "Bother those lights. We can't do without them, but they sure eat up money we need for things like fencing and runways. But, Beatty, what can I do for you?"

"I have an idea," I begin. "I was wondering if maybe Muddy Springs shouldn't put on an air show?"

To my own ears it sounds suddenly ridiculous, but Mr. Granger doesn't laugh. Instead he asks, "What makes you think so?"

"Well, it would be good publicity for the airport and might get more town people to think about air travel. And maybe some pilots who've never flown in here would find us. And it would be fun. Millie could be our crowd pleaser."

"Chasing sheep and running after trash!" Now Mr. Granger does laugh.

"We get people coming out on Sundays anyway, just to watch the regular planes. I bet hundreds would come for a real show. Mr. Granger, at fifty cents a person…think of the *revenue*!"

Its official name will be the First Annual Muddy Springs Airport Air Show. I'd like to take full credit for thinking it up, but to be honest, I learn the airport board was already considering holding one. My bringing it up just kind of spurred things on.

That, I guess, and my promise that Moss and I will do as much of the work as we can. For free, of course, though I hope that if the show does bring in some extra money, a little of it will get shared with Moss.

Word about the show spreads fast.

"I heard you was stirring things up out at that airfield," Joe calls when I bike by Joe's Texas Auto Parts. "Good for you."

Clo just shakes her head. "Beatty, I cannot believe the things you think to get into."

Grif's eyes sparkle. "An air show is what first got me realizing how I might turn knowing radios into a job."

And the kids in the malt shop offer every reaction from disbelief to applause.

Leila asks, "Dallas, why do you want to take on so much extra work?"

Julie Elise is enthusiastic. "Can I do something?" she asks. "I mean, be part of it?" while Milton chimes in with off-key fanfare.

"And," he says, "introducing the world-famous, Texas-famous, Muddy Springs–famous Julie Elise…"

"Sorry, you two," I tell them. "But the program doesn't call for vaudeville."

Even Kenzie gets caught up in the plans, suggesting that this pilot or that might be a good one to invite. And every plane that comes in for even an oil change, he wants buffed to sparkling just in case it winds up in the show.

One afternoon I clean the cockpit of a small private aircraft while Kenzie works on the motor. Its owner and a company pilot—old-timers, both of them—are killing time by grumbling about desk men who don't understand conditions aloft.

The company pilot is saying, "It was last February, dead of winter, and I told the Detroit dispatcher nobody could make Chicago that day. But he insisted the forecast called for clearing, and nothing would do but we load up the passengers and wait for a break in the clouds. Said he knew it was my call, but…"

"Kenzie," I ask, "you got something I can use as a scraper?"

"For what?"

"It looks like dried peanut butter."

"…The left engine wouldn't start," the pilot's saying. "Then a tire went flat…Mind, it was snowing, big, fluffy flakes."

Kenzie hands me up a screwdriver. "Where'd you find peanut butter?"

"Under where the long piece goes into the floor."

" 'Long piece'?" Kenzie says. "Beatty, don't you know the names of things yet?"

"…So," the pilot's saying, "we finally took off about two in the afternoon, five hours late. The weather getting worse by the minute. And choppy…It was soon reeking in that cabin, and the heater was stuck on high…Must have been eighty degrees near it, and ice inside the windows not ten feet away."

Kenzie leans over the edge of the cockpit where I'm working. "Now show me what you're talking about."

"This thingamabob."

"'Thingamabob'! Girl, that's the stick. The control column."

"What's it for?"

"For?!! To make your plane climb or descend, or to move the ailerons so your wings bank right or left. And those rudder pedals down there are for coordinating your turn."

We both pause to listen to the pilot.

"...getting so goopy I radioed down for an alternate course. And what did I get but an order to circle around *back* of Detroit to some emergency landing strip lined with smudge pots. We slipped in with conditions deteriorating so fast even the desk boys realized we were going to be socked in the rest of the day..."

"Served him right for trusting a durn forecast," Kenzie tells me.

"The funniest thing was," the pilot continues, "one of my passengers was a big shot from the home office. 'But I have business in Chicago,' he kept saying. I told him he was going to spend the night fifty miles farther away from Chicago than he'd started that morning."

"What's a smudge pot?" I whisper to Kenzie.

"Just a container with some fuel and a wick large enough to give off a big old tongue of flame. Not a bad way to mark a runway on a foggy night, if you don't mind the upkeep or the oily smoke. We had 'em here afore those field lights went in."

"You think that story was all true?" I whisper to Kenzie.

"With embellishments. Now, Beatty…," and Kenzie begins pointing to other things in the cockpit, naming them and telling me what they do. "See that throttle? It governs the engine's speed and power—gives you the thrust you need. Airplanes are complicated things, Beatty, and any maneuver takes working the controls together. Say you want to make a right turn, you've got to…"

I try hard to follow all he's saying, even while I ask myself, What's the use of trying to understand things I'm probably never going to see used, anyway? Grif will never let me take off in a plane again, and even if he does, Dad won't.

"Hey, Kenzie," says the pilot we've been listening to. He lights a pipe as he strolls over. "Are you trying to pack a whole course of aeronautics into that kid's head?"

"I ain't telling her anything Lindsey and Collin Donnough's daughter shouldn't know," Kenzie answers. "And you mind that NO SMOKING sign and get yourself outside where there's nothing flammable."

"I'm nowhere near—"

"Out! And don't hurry back. Your yarn swapping's making it hard for Beatty to concentrate."

Kenzie turns to the other guy, the one who owns the plane I've been cleaning. "You go on, too. Peanut butter!"

Chapter

16

$\mathcal{T}$HE AIR SHOW seems to be rushing toward us faster than we can do all we need to.

Mr. Granger has all the business details to arrange. He books pilots and their planes, figuring and refiguring how many tickets we'll have to sell before we start making more money than we'll have to pay for the acts. He arranges for insurance. Concessions. Where spectators will sit.

Since Grif is employed by an airline rather than by the airport, the show is not part of his job. Still he does a lot, including setting up a rented loudspeaker system.

Moss helps with that, saying, "I'll run it, long as no one expects me to do the announcing."

"You know," I suggest, "there are a couple of kids in town who just might be perfect."

And to give the others time to work on all they've taken on, I pitch in doing more and more of the airfield's regular chores.

I even sometimes help with the passenger planes, giving a

hand to copilots who have cargo to load or unload. One asks, "Since when does the company hire girls for this work?"

"I'm not doing it fast enough?" I ask. I grab a bundle of magazines and toss it through the door so quickly he jumps back to avoid being hit.

Kenzie, passing by, says, "Better watch out for Beatty. If the airline ever takes on female pilots, she might just be after your job!"

And Grif calls, "Kenzie, don't give her ideas."

But he winks at me.

Waiting to drop off to sleep that night, I think about that conversation.

Kenzie and Grif are proud of me.

While I've been too busy with all the things that need doing to think of myself, they've been thinking about me.

Of course, I know their talk is just plain silly. I can't imagine an airline ever hiring a female pilot.

But if my uncle and Kenzie can change their minds about what kind of girl I am, then maybe Dad might, too.

I hear the night mail flight coming in and mentally check off what Grif must be doing: getting ready to exchange mail bags and to top off the plane's gas tank, jobs Kenzie does for the milk run.

I wonder, Would knowing how I've become somebody needed at the airfield be enough to convince Dad I deserve a plane ride?

The engine sound gets louder as the mail plane nears town and then veers west.

I suppose there's a chance.

But perhaps...that's no longer all I want. Perhaps there's more that *I* can do, and just what that is will be up to me.

As though to show me what might be possible, the days before the air show bring three women to the airport. They're all connected to flying, though in different ways.

The first is Miss Betty Blanston, one of the company's brand-new stewardesses and the first ever to be on a plane landing in Muddy Springs.

She's gorgeous. Also really stylish, in a dark blue suit with a matching close-fitted cap. Because the flight's delayed on the ground an hour, I get to visit with her.

"How did you become a stewardess?" I ask. "Did you just think you'd like to do it and go apply?"

She laughs. "No. I was working in a hospital when an airline recruiter came offering all us nurses better wages than we were making there. Seven of us signed on before the hospital shut its doors to anyone who even looked like he was connected with aviation."

"Would you rather be a pilot?"

"Why, no," she answers. "Why ever would I?"

The next to come through is Amanda Winters, on her way to New York to take part in an aviation competition.

She's not *the* most famous woman flier in the world, but she's got a name in Texas.

Amanda Winters does not leave her plane to Kenzie and Moss's care alone. She supervises every drop of oil going in it, inspects the propeller blades herself, spends half an hour adjusting a rudder pedal just the way she wants it.

"She sure is picky," I whisper—to Kenzie, but Miss Winters hears me.

"And alive," she calls down.

The third is Annie Boudreau, who hasn't been around in quite a while because some state official hired her to take him to every air strip in Texas. "And there are dozens," she tells me. "All of them dusty. But it is about the steadiest work I've ever had."

We're sharing my lunch—some of Clo's chili—while we watch Moss service Annie's plane. It's as good a chance to talk with her as I'm likely to make.

"There's something I'd like to ask you about," I say. "Kenzie and others have been telling me about my mother—things she did that I never knew about before—but their stories don't make her seem real. Not like a person I can picture."

Annie looks at me, troubled. "I don't know what you want me to add." She seems thoughtful, though, and I wait for her to continue. But then her passenger shows up, and Moss signals that his work's done. Rising, Annie says, "We'll talk, Beatty. The first time I'm back here, we'll talk."

"When will that be?"

"I'll be over for the air show for sure."

As though we're not already busy enough, a dust storm a few days before the show causes us extra work.

It starts as a brown cloud on the western horizon. Sweeping our way in a sun-hiding murk that makes us have to turn on the field lights for the midmorning plane, it blows around everything loose outside and lays down a layer of grit on every surface in the terminal and hangar.

It terrifies Millie, who stays wrapped around my ankles for two solid hours, tripping me up every step I take.

"Millie," I say, reaching down to pet her, "you may be smart and talented, but you are also a coward."

Moss, helping Grif clean out the operations room, calls, "Might be she's smart enough to be acting."

"I think she was really scared."

We're interrupted by a radio transmission coming in and the telephone ringing both at the same moment. "I'll get the phone," I say.

It's an electrician from the lighting manufacturer, wanting to speak to Grif.

"He's not available at the moment." I reach for paper and a pencil. "May I take a message?"

"Tell him I'll come by this afternoon to look at that bad field light. Have him bring it in where I can get to it quick."

"I'll let him know."

I've hardly hung up, though, when the terminal door opens and a husband and wife come in wanting schedules and prices for flying to California. Clearing a space on the counter, I take out a system timetable and turn to the page showing coast-to-coast flights.

"There's a westbound plane every afternoon. You'll have only—let's see…one, two…six intermediate stops, and you'll be there in less than thirteen hours. A round-trip fare is one hundred forty-seven dollars and seventy-six cents."

Late in the afternoon, Grif and Moss and I are helping Kenzie with the hangar cleanup when a man appears at the doorway. He's carrying a toolbox and some sort of meter.

"Hey," he says, "you all didn't have to order a dust storm to prove you need your lights working. Where's that broken one?"

Grif breaks into a smile. "Are you ever welcome, even if you weren't expected. The one giving us the most trouble is on the boundary where—"

"Oh, Grif, I am so sorry," I say, taking from my pocket the note I'd written earlier. "I forgot to give you the message."

The man interrupts. "Don't you have the light pulled down and ready for me? I only have half an hour I can spend."

"But the whole layout needs work," Grif tells him. "Can you at least look at some temporary repairs I made?"

The man shakes his head. "Not today. If you'd had that one light ready for me, I might have fixed it, but trouble-shooting the entire system—that's several hours' work at least. Wish I'd known sooner that's what you needed: I could have switched today's work for tomorrow's."

"We've got an air show planned for Sunday," Grif tells him. "I sure hope the lights don't go down between now and then, not with all the planes that will be coming in."

"They're not likely to," the man says. "If the system was that iffy, this dust storm would have knocked it out. I'll come back next Wednesday or Thursday. Meanwhile, I guess you just keep changing bulbs as they burn out. Need some extras?"

After they've gone to get them from his truck, I ask Kenzie, "So you think we're going to be OK?"

"I'd say so, unless a lot stronger storm than the one we just had blows through. The forecast is for good weather."

"I thought you didn't trust forecasts."

"I don't," Kenzie says, "unless they agree with what my nose is telling me. But right now, my nose doesn't smell a hint of rain." He nods toward the push broom to indicate I ought to be using it. "And in the unlikely event both the forecast and my nose are wrong and those lights fail just when we need 'em—maybe we could put you out on the airfield with a couple of strong flashlights!"

Hearing Moss chuckle at the idea, I say, "Moss, too!"

"No, not Moss, too," Kenzie says. "He didn't forget to pass on any durn messages."

Chapter

17

THE WEATHER DOES hold. And Sunday! It's a clear-blue-sky, beautiful, not-too-hot, barely breezy day like doesn't come once in a hundred Augusts in Texas

A banner that Clo made—AIR SHOW TODAY—flutters between the hangar and the terminal.

The show's not supposed to start until two-thirty, but by noon people from town are arriving in a steady stream. Some stake out seats on the temporary grandstand. Others spread blankets on the airport grounds and open picnic baskets and lemonade jugs. Lots more just pull their cars off the road and roll down their convertible tops or perch on their hoods.

As starting time approaches it looks like all Muddy Springs is at the airport, and a lot of people from other towns, too.

The group parked along Airfield Road upsets Mrs. Granger. "They're not paying," she says. She has to shout to be heard over the noise of airplane motors being turned over, of pilots calling greetings to each other, of marching-band music pouring from loudspeakers. "Nobody's supposed to watch for free."

But Mr. Granger is too happy, excited, and busy to mess with a few freeloaders. "It's a success," he tells her. "Sweet, our air show is a success!"

"Grif," I say, as we give pilots carbon copies of the timetable I've typed up, "how can he say the show's a success when it hasn't even started yet?"

But my uncle asks, "Are you sure it hasn't?"

A wave of laughter comes from the grandstand, and looking to see why, I spot Millie. She's out in front of the crowd, performing all by herself, tossing a ball and then chasing it. Sitting up and clapping her front paws. Taking a bow. Turning and leaping and flipping over and then waiting for more applause.

The crowd loves it.

"Grif!" I exclaim. "She's not supposed to be on yet. Her act is playing Monkey in the Middle with Moss and me, trying to get a ball away from us—"

"Beatty," he tells me, "I think you and Moss better leave crowd pleasing to an expert."

Mr. Granger approaches the microphone stand, and as though Millie understands what a good introduction is, she covers the apron in a lightning series of half somersaults and winds up jumping into Mr. Granger's arms.

He staggers back but hangs on. "Ladies and gentlemen," he says, "I'm honored to present an exhibition team from the army, opening our spectacular First Annual Muddy Springs Airport Air Show."

Millie leans in toward the megaphone and howls, and every person in sight is clapping when three military planes soar up from the airfield, circle, and fly into the distance.

They're followed right away by Annie taking off in *Gold Lightning*.

Julie Elise's voice on the loudspeaker system tells the crowd, "The army planes will be back, but first, pilot Annie Boudreau will show what she can do. She'll demonstrate some patterns, make a climbing turn called a chandelle, and then show you what the word *spin* really means. Watch for a vertical roll followed by a loop and a barrel roll."

"And after her," breaks in Milton's voice, "look for those Army Air Corps planes to return with some spectacular precision flying."

Overhead the gold stripes of Annie's plane flash as she traces a tight, twisting figure eight. She layers on dizzying patterns, one after another, each just a little higher than the one before, until it's hard to know which she's flying and which are just lingering in my mind.

What must it feel like, to be able to do that?

I'm startled to realize that I'm pressing my foot into the grass as though I'm the one pushing down on a rudder pedal. I struggle to picture the actions: When Annie's pushing on the right pedal, she must also be pulling back the stick and moving it right.

By the time I get the figure eights figured out, Annie's flying off in another direction, moving from maneuver to maneuver so fast I give up trying to do more than just lose myself in the joy of watching.

I meet her plane when she lands and help her out of a parachute that turns her walk into a waddle. "You were wonderful! All those acrobatics!"

She says, "A few stunts, maybe, but the routine was mostly just a fancy way to show skills any good pilot practices."

"Then what's the parachute for?"

"Another good practice—being prepared in case something goes wrong."

A pack of little kids gathers about Annie, a couple of them even holding out autograph books, and several adults want to shake her hand. Even a pilot I've heard make snide comments about women not belonging on ships, either sea or air, gives her a thumbs-up.

I start away but hear Annie call, "Beatty, let's find some cold soda." I feel myself blushing with the pleasure of being singled out. Is it because she's remembered her promise that we'll talk?

We buy the drinks but don't see a good spot to settle down with them, not with the crowds everywhere. Then I get an idea: "I know one unclaimed place with a great view."

When Annie realizes I mean for us to climb up on the terminal roof, she throws back her head in laughter. "Oh, Beatty," she says, helping me drag over the ladder, "in some ways you are *so* like your mother!"

She's still laughing when we perch on the huge S in the painted MUDDY SPRINGS, and I wait for her to stop before asking, "Now will you tell me about her?"

Annie turns to look at me. "That flying I just did—I was trying to *show* your mother to you. That's the way Lindsey would have flown, if she'd lived. Lindsey's flying would have been even better."

A tumble of questions occur to me, but my throat's suddenly too tight for asking them. Instead, I listen to Julie Elise announce the first of the afternoon's air circus acts, and Annie and I watch a biplane fly low before the crowd. A tiny figure climbs from the cockpit.

Hushed *ohhhhh*s drift among the spectators as the figure struggles for balance and then, reaching from one handhold to the next, paces out to the end of a wing. There the wing-walker stops, kneels, and straightens into a headstand.

"Can you imagine!" I say, as the crowd breaks into applause. "That does look dangerous."

"It is," Annie answers. "Just as dangerous as when your mother and I tried it. It was crazy, but we wanted money to buy Jennys from the war surplus the government was selling off."

"My mother was a *wing-walker*! And you, too?"

"Not me," Annie says. "I tried it just once, tied to a safety line, Lindsey's instructions from her own first time ringing in my ears. 'There's nothing to it,' she said. 'Just step from rib to rib and don't put a foot through the canvas.' I went about half a yard before deciding I'd earn airplane money some other way."

"But my *mother*! *She* was a wing-walker!"

"Briefly, back when you were a baby," Annie says. "Until your father found out. It was one of the few times he ever said *no* to her, and he made it up by helping finance her Jenny himself. Against his better judgment, he said. They were already arguing…"

Annie looks at me curiously. "You really don't know anything about your mother?"

I shake my head. "Dad hardly talks about her. It was Kenzie who told me she was a pilot."

"Your mother," Annie says slowly, as though trying to pick just what's most important for me to know, "was like those gold stripes on my airplane, always seeming to flash more blinding the higher she climbed. She was my best friend from the day we met at the field where we were both taking flying lessons.

"Had to be friends, I guess, since we were the only females around, no folks of our own, both of us paying our way with the end of money our parents had left us. I liked your mother even though I couldn't keep up with her. Even then I knew when to be frightened."

Annie breaks off to watch two planes compete in flying laps above a barrel on the airfield. Then she picks up her thoughts at a different place. "Your father...Beatty, I can still see how he used to look at Lindsey, as though he was dazzled by her brightness."

"He doesn't talk like he was dazzled by her," I say. "The few times he has mentioned my mother, it's been more like he was angry."

Annie, folding and unfolding the ends of her long silk scarf, is silent for several moments. Then she says, "The year after you were born your mother saw a chance to win an air race. It was one of those contests where flyers all start at one place and head for another, and the winner's whoever gets there first.

"Other contestants had bigger, faster planes than Lindsey did, but she had a risky northern route planned that she thought might even the odds. Your father—all of us—tried to talk her out of it, but this time she wouldn't listen."

I hear the grandstand erupt with cheers, but nothing could make me take my eyes from Annie's face.

"So what happened?"

"A slow-moving weather front rolled in a few hours into the race. It grounded most of the pilots, but your mother put down just long enough to refuel and then took off again into a thick overcast. She told a mechanic she couldn't be worried by a little autumn sleet, that she'd climb above it and get ahead of the front. 'There's sun up there someplace,' she said.

"Three days later searchers found your mother where she'd made a forced landing on an ice field in Canada. She was barely alive."

About to die of pneumonia. That must be when Dad took her and me to San Antonio.

Annie unties the long scarf from her neck and holds it out. "Your mother and I bought matching scarves the day we soloed. I don't know what happened to hers, but perhaps you'd like this one."

"Thank you," I tell her, "but I don't think so. What I don't understand is how my mother could do something everybody knew was dangerous. I guess this sounds selfish, but...didn't she care about me?"

That gets a chuckle from Annie. "Oh, she did, Beatty. Lindsey talked about you and carried your picture with her everywhere. She'd swing into one of those creaking old wood hangars where a woman was about as welcome as fog, and make every man in it admire you!"

The idea of my mother showing baby photos to a hangar full of Kenzies makes me laugh, though I ask, "But where would I be? Who'd be taking care of me?"

"Your father, if he was home. Sometimes I'd have you, or some other friend your mother trusted. She'd leave pages of instructions about your care."

Groping through ideas new to me, I say, "Maybe that helps explain why Dad's the way he is. Maybe he's still mad because part of what he loved was the daring that killed her."

Annie looks startled. Then she says, "Beatty, you just may be a very wise young woman."

But then, thinking about *all* Annie's told me, I burst out,

"How can I be so proud of my mother and at the same time feel so *angry*?"

And now it's Annie who's laughing. "What you've done, Beatty, is bump into the puzzle of Lindsey Donnough—the same one anybody who loved her came up against: how she could have been both so wonderful and—forgive me, Beatty—so foolish at the same time."

This time, when applause sweeps through the crowd, we both look to see what's causing it. There's a skit beginning in front of a sign that says NEW YORK. A pilot slings a bag with a big AIR MAIL sign into the cockpit of a small plane, climbs in, and takes off.

Meanwhile, another man with a bag, labeled GROUND MAIL, steps into the cardboard cutout of a train. He moves it just a little way before reaching the end of wood tracks. The mail plane takes off, and the man on the ground transfers his bag to a truck.

"Did you dream that up, Beatty?" Annie asks.

"I painted the signs," I tell her.

Overhead the mail plane swoops by, while on the ground the mail gets moved from truck to wagon to horse to mule and, finally, to a sled behind Millie. Millie wriggles out of her harness and trots off just as the air-mail plane taxis to a stop in front of a sign saying LOS ANGELES.

"Pretty good," Annie says. "And not too far from the truth."

She again holds out her silk scarf. "Want to change your mind?"

"Maybe I'll at least borrow it," I say, "while I do some thinking."

Now the army planes that began the show soar into a finale,

and Julie Elise's voice over the loudspeaker says, "Beatty Donnough, Mr. Granger wants you down in front of the grandstand."

Milton's voice in the background can be heard urging, "Go on, Moss. He wants you down there, too."

Mr. Granger tells the crowd that if they've liked the air show, they should give Moss and me a round of applause, and they do.

Though, of course, Millie thinks the clapping is for her. She prances and bows and, to tell the truth, judging from how the audience is laughing, she's probably got it right.

Chapter

18

*T*HAT EVENING CLO and Grif and I lean back in the lawn chairs outside our cabin, and I wonder if the two of them are feeling the way I do, hardly able to believe this day is over.

It has been so full, and such a *finish*.

I finally understand what happened to my mother all those years ago, and in a way I'm not so much surprised as relieved. It makes her a real person, with parts I can love and parts I don't. The way Moss feels about his mother, I guess.

The understanding gives me a new view of my dad, one that suggests why he wasn't more honest with his family before I was born. And it helps lessen my disappointment that he didn't come to today's show even though I asked him specially.

But settling my parents' story, important as it is, seems just a gentle ripple in all my contentment.

"Could any day have been more perfect?" I ask.

"It would be hard to imagine one," Clo answers. She reaches across to take Grif's hand. "Grif, did you tell Beatty your news?"

"What news?" I ask.

"That it's definite the station manager I've been filling in for won't be returning," Grif says, "and that Mr. Granger was so pleased with how things went today he offered to call the airline and urge them to give the job to me permanently."

"Grif, that's wonderful!"

"I reminded him the show was your doing, and Moss's—"

Clo interrupts to say, "And it means we'll be able to stop this tourist-court living and move into a house. Maybe get one with an extra bedroom, so that if you really do want..."

I catch my breath. "Clo...Do you mean...Are you inviting me...Really?"

Clo and Grif both nod, looking pleased and shyly private. And then, as though keeping the rest of their news a secret is more than Clo can do, she says, "Beatty, I'd like your new cousin to grow up with you around every single day."

"My new— CLO!"

I fling my arms around my aunt to hug her and her baby-to-be, both.

"Careful!" she says as we all laugh.

But after a moment Grif cautions, "About your staying with us for good—we'll have to clear it with your father."

"I don't know," Dad says the next morning. His voice is hard to hear over the crackle of long-distance phone lines. "You write what it is you want to do."

"To live with Clo and Grif."

"There's Fanny and Maud. They'd miss you."

"And I'd miss them, but I can visit. Dad, please."

"I don't know why you want to go changing what's worked all these years, Beatty. I think you just better..."

121

Static covers his next words, and I wait for the noise to lessen before asking, "Dad, won't you please come here so we can at least talk about it?"

"I don't—"

"School starts next week, so I need to know. And there's something else I want to talk to you about…just to straighten out…"

"Beatty, I can't…"

"Please, Dad. It's important."

"What is? This connection's no good. Look, maybe I can try to catch a ride in on tomorrow night's mail plane if there's an extra seat. I'll see."

The rest of Monday is mostly taken up with getting the airport back to rights. In the morning I lug a sack from one end of the lawn to the other and all up and down the road, collecting trash, while Moss works with Kenzie to knock down the grandstand.

And then, when I go looking for Moss at lunchtime, he's gone. "He went to town," Kenzie says.

I see Moss return a while later, but by then I'm helping with a million passenger chores, and I never do get free to talk to Moss the rest of the afternoon. Which about kills me, when I've got so many things to tell him.

At dinner Clo says she's been making arrangements to see her sisters. "Fanny and I are going to catch early buses to Maud's tomorrow. We'll be there in time for lunch."

"You're going all the way to Waco to eat?" Grif asks.

"No. To talk about the baby," Clo answers. "And I can explain better about wanting Beatty to stay with us. I don't want their feelings hurt."

Grif shakes his head as though Clo and her sisters are still sometimes too much for him. "And you can't just write?"

Tuesday morning I wave to Clo as we wait for her bus to pull away from Muddy Springs Drug.

She leans out a window to ask, "Are you sure you won't come? You'll be by yourself here all day and evening, what with Grif planning to work through dinner. I won't be back before midnight."

"I'm sure, Clo," I tell her. "You all can talk about me better if I'm not around. Just please see the talk comes out the way I want it to!"

After she leaves, I find Julie Elise and Leila and poke around town with them awhile.

Grif has given me the day off—a thank-you, he said, for the air show and for helping clean up after. He meant so well by it that I couldn't tell him I'd rather work.

Or, at least, that I'd rather be out at the airfield, where I can see Moss. It's funny, but for all my insisting he's just a casual friend, he's become more than that.

Anyway, I have a hard time getting interested in Julie Elise's and Leila's chatter, and after lunch at the malt shop I head back to the tourist court.

In the cabin I check the icebox, thinking I'll take Grif's supper out to him if he's forgotten it, but he hasn't.

I notice, though, a couple of chickens that Clo's got all cut up and ready for frying. *I could offer everybody something better for supper than cold sandwiches...*

A moment later I'm reaching for a skillet.

When I arrive at the airport in the late afternoon, picnic basket strapped across my bike handles, I go first to the terminal. Grif is in the operations room, shaking his head, reading a dispatch as it clatters off the teletypewriter.

"What's the matter?" I ask.

"Just trying to make sense of contradictory weather reports. Some of the rural stations are reporting hail here and thunderclouds there, but the official word is that skies are fair all across Texas."

"The sky looks OK right now."

"That can change. What smells so good?"

"Fried chicken. I'll set you out a plate. And Grif? If Dad does come in on the mail plane, when you two get back to the tourist court will you have him come say hello? I'm going to wait up."

"It'll be late."

"That's OK. I want to see him, and I'm going to wait up for Clo, anyway."

"Moss, Kenzie!" I call, going in the hangar.

"Moss ain't here," Kenzie answers, climbing down from Annie Boudreau's plane. His limp seems more pronounced than usual as he walks toward me. "Seemed fair to give him the day off, seeing as you got one."

"But I brought you both fried chicken!"

"Well, him being gone won't keep me from enjoying it! Any drumsticks?"

As I pick them out, I mention that my dad may be coming in on the night mail flight.

"*If* it comes in," Kenzie says. "My bum leg and my nose both say a storm's on the way."

"So do some of the farmers who call in, but the weather service says flying is going to be fine."

"There's weathermen who wouldn't know rain if they looked out a window and saw water."

I KNOW CLO DOESN'T want me going out to Moss's place—"Beatty," she says, "it's just not a good idea"—but I've got all this food left. Clo wouldn't want me to waste it.

So, I tell myself, *go put it in the cabin icebox before it spoils.*

But honestly, it's as if my bicycle has a will of its own. I intend to turn the handlebars toward town, I truly do, but somehow I end up pedaling north.

I find Moss near the creek, working at a table he's put together of scrap wood. He's writing a letter but sets it aside when he sees me.

A grin spreading on his face, he exclaims, "Beatty! What are you doing here?"

"I've come to have a picnic supper with you. I've got fried chicken."

"Really?" Moss lifts the basket top. "Great!"

He's all for eating right away, but I suggest, "Moss, let's

make it a true picnic. We can hike up the bluff and eat on top—
I've never been up there."

The bluff is higher and harder to climb than I'd have
guessed, but it's worth every step. From where its highest part
juts out in a flat ledge, the view is of land stretching miles and
miles to a curved horizon.

"This must be how things look from an airplane," I say.

"Sort of," Moss answers. "But from really way up the land
seems kind of checkered."

We talk and talk, and by the time we're done eating the sun
has become a blinding half-ball in a western blaze of copper and
pink, while to the east the sky has begun shading darker and
darker to dusk.

I've run down all the things I wanted to tell Moss, and he's
as excited and pleased for me as I hoped he'd be.

But now he says, "Beatty, things are goin' to change for me,
too. I got a letter from Ma yesterday. She wrote that my pa has
got the government work he was after and thinks I can sign on,
too."

"But...I didn't know you were thinking of leaving here,
Moss. Where to?"

"Pa's planting trees in Montana, so I reckon Ma's thinking
up there. Only, the other thing is Mr. Granger's offered me a
regular job at the airport. I guess between extra shop work and
what the show did there's money comin' in."

"So you can stay! Moss, that is so much better."

"He says I can move into the little upstairs room at the terminal. I'd keep the grounds and help Kenzie part-time. It'd let
me go back to school."

"And once you finish high school, Moss, then maybe you can go on to really learn about radio work and—"

He seems more troubled than excited. "What bothers me," he says, "is joining Pa or this new conservation corps outfit for young men, I'd likely make more money than here. Ma expects it."

"Moss, I know you've got to help your family, and I don't mean to be disrespectful to them," I argue, "but maybe you need to do different than what they expect of you. More, perhaps, but different…"

Moss nods. "That's what I was trying to write Ma when you got here. It ain't a easy thing to say."

Then he grins and corrects himself. "Isn't. *An* easy."

It seems the most natural thing in the world when Moss puts his arm around me. And when I tell him, "I guess I ought to be getting back," Moss agrees, "You're right," but we continue sitting together.

Bit by bit the sun drops out of sight, the streaking western clouds turning a dark, inky purple and the sky overhead deepening through all the blues to charcoal. A star pops out, and then another.

And as though the land is trying to keep pace, a light appears far off to our left, and then one to our right, at the very edge of the horizon.

"Look, Moss. Those must be airway beacons. It's like we really are in a plane, with one light behind us and one in front. Annie says that sometimes you can see a whole string of beacons stretched out to guide your way."

"On clear nights, maybe. But I'd put my faith in radio range signals."

"Annie says things can go wrong flying the beam, too… Moss, do you think everything's going to turn out all right for us?"

"Who knows?" he answers. "But I hope so."

A breeze picks up, one so suddenly cool that I shiver, and Moss tightens his arm around me. Annie's scarf, the one she gave me, flutters against my face, and Moss laughs and brushes it free.

Together we watch Muddy Springs become a distant electric glow and see the airport lights come on atop the terminal and hangar. A revolving beacon sweeps white…green…white… green.

Even after the moon comes up, neither of us says any more about leaving.

And then other airport lights come on: red ones that warn of the pole line, and perimeter floods that illuminate the landing field.

"Moss…Are those on because the night mail plane's due in?" I ask, suddenly panicked. "I've got to get back to the tourist court before the others do."

"Come on," Moss says, on his feet in an instant.

We're scrambling to gather up the picnic things when a wind gust yanks a napkin from my hands. And moments later, far in the west, lightning streaks in a tall bolt. I count to twenty—it's an even four miles off—before thunder rumbles. "You think that rain's coming this way?"

"Might be."

The first drops hit before we reach the base of the bluff, and by the time we get back to the caboose the rain is pelting down.

"You want to wait it out inside?" Moss asks.

"I can't. If I'm not at the cabin when Grif gets there, he'll be worried sick. And Dad...if he comes in and finds me missing, he'll really be upset. I've got to try to get to the airport."

"Beatty, no plane's going to fly in here, not in this weather. But come on, I'll go with you."

"You don't need to," I tell him. "Besides, I've got my bicycle."

Lightning strikes, this time only a count of eleven away.

Moss says, "You can't be hanging on to a metal bike in an electric storm. And you ain't goin' alone."

We take off holding hands, half running, half sliding over newly slick ground. Soon the rain is beating so hard on my face I can hardly see, and I'm out of breath and my side hurts and I'm worried. In fact, I'd be plain miserable, except I don't think I've ever had more fun. I feel silly and happy, and I can't stop laughing.

Half way down Airfield Road, Moss suddenly halts.

"What is it?" I ask.

"Just this," he says, kissing me. And it's not just a peck on my cheek, either, though I hardly have time to kiss back before he breaks off to pull me along again, running.

The storm moves faster than we do, blocking out the moon but lighting the land in jagged lines so frequent we can make our way by them. We're still a long half mile from the airport when the strikes begin coming so close together that it's impossible to tell which bolt goes with which *crack*.

Something nearby snaps and rips, a splitting tree maybe.

Suddenly I remember Millie.

"Moss!" I exclaim, shouting to be heard over the noise, "Where's the dog? She must be scared to death."

But instead of answering he tells me, "Listen, Beatty. Do you hear a motor?"

"You told me nothing would fly through this." A second later, though, I hear coming from behind us the unmistakable sound of an airplane engine. "You don't think it's the mail plane, do you?"

Just then the landing field floodlights flicker several times and go dark, along with the red obstruction lights.

"It's that bad line," I tell Moss. "Grif's jury-rigged fix must not have held up to the storm."

The sound of the airplane engine gets fainter and then disappears.

"It must be going on to another landing field," I say.

Moss and I hurry along as fast as we can, but we're still a good piece from the airport when we see a lightning bolt appear to touch earth right there. Instantly the revolving beacon and building lights go dark.

"The power must of been knocked out," Moss says.

And it's then that the engine sound returns, this time over to the right and behind us. It gets louder and then again fades out in the direction it came from.

"Moss!" I say as a sudden fear hits me. "Do you think that plane is lost? That it can't find the airfield? *Could it be the mail plane?*"

For long moments strong waves of wind keep us from

moving forward at all. When they die down, the rain doubles in force.

"Moss," I urge, "hurry!"

And then, as quickly as the storm came on us, it lets up, becoming no more than single raindrops and a light breeze by the time we reach the airport drive.

20

$\mathcal{T}$HE LOW CLOUD cover hangs on, though, keeping the night dark enough that Moss and I almost bump into the terminal door, which is standing half-open.

My uncle wouldn't have left without closing up.

"Grif?" I call, not getting any answer. "I'll fetch the flashlight he keeps behind the counter."

Feeling my way across the room, I knock over two or three objects before my hand closes on the light. I swing its beam over scattered papers and glass from a broken back window.

"Do you think Grif was still here when the storm hit so hard?" I ask.

"I don't know," Moss answers. "But we best get on the radio in case that plane comes back. Though with the power down, we got to get the generator going first."

Behind the building, I hold the flashlight and try to shield Moss from the dregs of the storm while he sets the generator's choke and swings the crank a couple of times. Then he switches on the ignition and turns the handle one more full turn. The engine makes a single *chuunk* and dies. He turns it again... *chuunk*...and again...*chuunk*...before finally it catches.

We run back inside, to the operations room.

"This is Muddy Springs," Moss says, twisting radio dials. "Can you hear me?"

The loudspeaker is emitting static so bad that Moss switches it off, and I jam my face next to his trying to hear a voice in his earphones.

"Any aircraft around, please answer," Moss says.

One disconnected part of me thinks that this probably isn't even legal. Moss doesn't have a license for transmitting.

But all the rest of me is focused on the faint sound I'm hearing, Dad's voice trying to answer.

But that can't be. Even if it is the mail plane up there, it must be the pilot talking. Dad is coming in as a passenger.

I know Dad's voice.

"Muddy Springs," I hear. "...read? Can...read?"

"That's my father!" I tell Moss. Dad is almost incomprehensible in a crescendo of static and buzz and whine.

"Captain Donnough, come in," Moss says. "This is Muddy Springs."

"...Springs?" Dad says again. "...bearings..."

"Captain Donnough? I think you're somewheres northwest of the Muddy Springs Airport. Can you pick up the radio beam?"

The static gets louder.

"Moss," I say, clutching his arm, "with the electricity out, is the radio beacon even sending signals?"

"I don't know, Beatty. I don't think the generator powers much more than this set."

Static from the radio grows louder.

"Captain, can you hear?" Moss repeats. "I think you're northwest, that's northwest, of Muddy Springs."

Something pops inside the receiver and the sound from the set goes dead. The glow around the rims of the dials becomes faint and then disappears altogether.

"The generator must of quit," Moss says.

I run to the main room so I can look outside. The rain has completely stopped and the sky is lightening up a bit, but it's still far too overcast and dark for me to see anything in it.

We try the telephone, but that's dead, too.

"If we could just call Grif or Kenzie," I say, "one of them might have an idea what to do."

"Maybe the hangar phone's still OK," Moss says.

The hangar doors stand partway open, and inside there's another chaos of knocked-over equipment and scattered paper.

Again, I realize that open doors are wrong—the wind might have blown them off their tracks but not rolled them sideways.

Before I can think more about that, though, something slams into my legs.

Then Millie is all over me, shaking wet dog fur and nipping at my hands. "Not now," I tell her.

But she's insistent, tugging on me, pulling me to where the workbench with its tall shelves lies on its side.

"What?" I ask just before the flashlight shows me Grif. He's crumpled beside a broken wood crate, and blood is running from a cut on his forehead. The receiver from the wall telephone is clutched in his hand, its cord torn loose.

"Moss!" I yell. "Come here fast! Grif's been hurt."

135

"Grif?" Moss says, bending over him. "Beatty, that crate must of come down on his head."

My uncle wakes, blinking and dazed, in the flashlight beam; comes to, fretting and anxious. "Why are the lights off? Night plane due in…radioed…low on fuel."

He tries to struggle to his feet, but his left leg buckles and he collapses. "Have to bring Collin in…"

"Grif?" I ask. "Grif?"

"He's passed out again, Beatty," Moss says.

"But he can't…Moss…my dad is on that plane…"

Help. The thought circles and stalls. *We've got to get help, and there's no one to give it to us.*

"You stay here with your uncle," Moss says, "while I go try to get the generator fixed."

"Here," I tell him. "You take the flashlight."

"Keep it. I just spotted Kenzie's."

And then Moss is gone and I'm holding a handkerchief to the cut on Grif's head, trying to comprehend what's going on.

That's my father up there, not sure exactly where he is, and even if he flies directly overhead there's no way he can see the landing field. But if he comes in anyway and hits that power line…He wouldn't want to land blind, but, running out of fuel, he might not have a choice.

I try to think as he must be thinking. He might have seen town lights, and Moss's contact would have confirmed they were Muddy Springs's. Taking his bearings from them, using his compass, Dad would know about where the airport would be.

But *about where*'s not good enough. Not with the field un-lighted and the weather what it is.

And then suddenly, as though he's right here saying the

words again, I hear Kenzie joke about putting me out on the field with a couple of strong flashlights.

Flashlights wouldn't do any good, but...

One after another, the stories I've been listening to all summer speed by, bits jumping out: There was one about how, years ago, a whole set of hangars and workshops went up in flames. "Wooden buildings and fabric skins on the planes. The fire started in a drum of drained fuel."

And that company pilot told about the storm out of Detroit, how he had to land on a runway marked off with smudge pots.

"A cylinder with some fuel and a wick," Kenzie said. *"A big old tongue of flame."*

My mind racing, I pause just long enough to whisper, "Grif? You doing OK?"

He stirs. "Yes. But...plane...Need to bring it..."

"I've thought of a way," I tell him, trying to sound a confidence I don't feel. What I feel is afraid.

Taking the broken crate with me, I run outside, searching until my flashlight beam picks up the trash can blown a distance from where it should be.

Jamming the crate pieces inside, I drag the can to the far end of the ramp, running and stumbling until I slide onto the mud of the landing field.

Leaving the can at the end of the worn path that most planes take, I hurry back to the hangar, this time getting matches and loading my arms with shop rags and newspapers to stuff in with the broken crate pieces.

My final trip is to the big container where drained crankcase oil is stored. I put some into a five-gallon can and then run to pour it over everything in the trash barrel.

The plane returns briefly as I pull out the matches. Frantic as I am to get a fire going, part of my mind registers that the engine sound is coming from the south, where the power line is.

Quickly I pull out several of the oil-soaked rags and drop them a good distance away. Turning back, I wonder, *Will this explode when I light it?*

Crouching beside the trash can, I strike a match, reach above me, and drop it in.

Nothing happens, and I realize it must have blown out.

A second match does also, but before lighting a third I move around so the trash can is between me and the breeze.

This time the fire catches, though there's no explosion at all, only a brief flare-up of glow. When I stand back to look, I see a small flame spreading along the edges of a newspaper. It wavers, threatens to go out, and then expands across an oily spot. Then a whole thick section of paper catches.

I don't wait longer but bring more things to feed the blaze until, suddenly, I have the bonfire I wanted, flames shooting out the trash can.

It's hard to tell how much light they throw off. The terminal and hangar still appear only as looming, almost invisible shapes, but maybe that's because the flames have taken my night vision. Maybe, from the sky...

And at least I've got one end of a landing path marked. But I need to mark its side so Dad doesn't blunder onto that power line, and if I can, I need to get a light going way down on the opposite end.

Grabbing up the oil-soaked rags I pulled out, I run diagonally up the airfield, trying to follow the carved-out runway. Making my way by flashlight, I slip and slide across the mud, stumbling and catching myself time and again, and I soon lose all idea of how much farther I have to go.

Then I hear the engine sound approaching again. For just an instant I take my eyes off the ground, but that's enough to send me sprawling onto it...not onto dry stubble now but into slick mud, but it's the same, feels the same as it did when I fell and *Gold Lightning* almost hit me.

Overhead, the plane flies so near and low that I glimpse a flash of bonfire reflected in its underside. Then the sound retreats again, going toward the far end of the field.

Dad's spotted the buildings. He's going to turn ninety degrees and turn again and try to land on this field that I'm in the middle of.

It's what I want him to do, but still I'm so scared that I want to huddle where I am. Getting up is the hardest thing I've ever done, but I do it, and I run as long as the airplane's sound is disappearing, just stopping to set two small rag fires along the way.

Then, when I hear the plane turn toward me, I yank aside some wet weeds, drop the remaining rags on the cleared patch, and light them. And then I listen....

The engine sounds very close, loud and racing toward me, and I think...I *think*...I can see the plane coming in low at the far end of the field. Then there's a loud sputtering that ends in sudden quiet. *What—*

Now I fling myself to the ground purposely, close to the little fire, my cheek pressed in the mud as I watch a dark shape touch down. Dad makes a rough, bouncing landing, and when the plane finally stops, it's not a hundred yards away.

Running out, I fling muddy arms around him as he climbs down from the cockpit. "I am so glad you're safe!" I cry.

We're still hugging each other, me repeating, "I was so

afraid—so scared you'd not find the airfield or you'd run into the buildings or the power line—so scared you wouldn't see the fires I—," when suddenly the floodlights come on atop the terminal and hangar roofs. Other, inside lights make yellow squares of doors and windows, and two sets of headlights come up the airport driveway.

"Oh," I say. "You could just have waited."

"No, I couldn't," Dad says. "I glided onto the airfield on an empty tank—" He breaks off, startled. "You set those fires? You were running around out on that field?"

"I was so afraid. For you, but for myself, too. I knew you couldn't see me in the dark, and..."

Chapter

21

M Y ANSWER MAKES him furious. "And you went out there anyway, took a chance on getting killed? I told you before, only fools take risks."

Then Dad notices the scarf I'm wearing, the soggy silk gleaming in the light now reaching us. He lifts one end and spreads it. "Your mother had one like this."

"I know."

Dad jerks back at that. "Then you must know why I don't want you to be like her. She thought she could do whatever she wanted, that she was above danger—"

"Dad, I'm not my mother."

"—and she wouldn't listen to warnings, didn't hear what anyone tried to tell her."

"But I do listen. If I didn't, I wouldn't have understood how much danger you were in, or known to mark the field with fires, or how to."

Dad shakes his head, a small, quick movement, as though he's clearing away far-off thoughts to make room for what I'm saying. Leaning back against the airplane, he tells me, "No, you're not your mother."

Then he looks down, rounds his shoulders, almost seems to shrink as he draws inside himself. "But Clo was right. You're not me, either, turning away from what frightens you."

"But that's not fair to you," I tell him. "You flew in here tonight, despite the storm, because I needed you. What did you do, take the mail route yourself when you found there wasn't room for a passenger?"

"It is fair, Beatty." Dad shakes his head again, and now his voice sounds both rueful and proud. "Guess I'll be hearing for years to come how my daughter brought me to a safe landing."

"So I'll be part of your hangar flying?" I ask, knowing the answer is *yes*.

What I also think, though I don't say it, is that tonight's happenings will also become front-porch talk: a story to tell when Dad's visiting, family talk while we're waiting for some summer evening to cool. This will be one more story to tie us together before Dad leaves again, flies on to the next place.

Suddenly I realize that the ceiling is lifting and the overcast is breaking into fast-moving clouds that circle and spin, cover the moon, and then part to spill light. It is beautiful up there....

But it must be so lonely, I think, *if the sky is all the home a person has.*

"Beatty," Dad says, tipping back my chin, smiling as though he's done with deep thinking for one night, "you look moonstruck."

A moment later there's a shout: Kenzie yelling, "You OK out there?"

Dad and I reach the hangar just as Grif is being helped to an ambulance. He's hobbling, one ankle immobilized against a splint, and worrying aloud about who'll meet Clo's bus, but he breaks into a huge grin when he sees us. "Collin," he says, "that was close."

"It was," Dad answers. "But Beatty saved me."

"And Moss did," I add. "That was Moss on the radio."

I turn to him. "The telephone must have started working again so you could call Kenzie and the ambulance?"

Annie's little roadster pulls up, causing Kenzie to say, "Yeah, Moss called me. And it looks like he called all Muddy Springs."

Moss nods. "Just about."

Millie nudges my hand and whines.

"Yes, Millie," I tell her. "You helped, too."

After smothering out the fire in the trash can and being sure the smaller ones have stopped burning, we follow the ambulance to town. Kenzie drives his own car and the rest of us go in Annie's, Moss included. Dad offered to share his cabin for the night, saying, "It'll be dry, anyway," and Moss, soaked to the skin, said, "Thanks."

Annie plans aloud. "These two should change clothes first. You've got something Moss can put on?"

Dad, in the front seat, nods.

"And then we'll meet Clo's bus and take her on to the hospital so she can see for herself that Grif's all right."

Moss and I are snuggled close together in the rumble seat, and about the time we turn off Airfield Road onto the highway he takes my hand.

———

There's a lot of confusion in the next couple of hours, and I don't hear the whole of anybody's conversation. Over and over, though, everyone tells everyone else about the airport electricity going out, and about how I brought Dad's plane in with a bonfire.

I do find time for whispering to Clo, "How'd it go?"

She squeezes my arm. "We're a family, angel! Maud and Fanny send their love, but Grif and I have you for good."

There's one odd moment when I notice Clo and Annie together, really the first time they've had much chance to talk. I get the impression they're taking stock of each other and that each approves of what she sees.

Then the moment's over, and they're again a part of the noisy excitement. Mr. Granger, who's come down to the hospital with his clothes pulled on over his pajamas, calls Moss and me heroes. "Aren't these kids something?" he says to whoever will listen. "I bet Fort Worth itself doesn't have any kids like these."

After a while, it makes me uneasy, taking credit for helping in an emergency I partly caused. Finally, about the time Mr. Granger is wondering aloud how early somebody can call the newspaper, I ask, "Please, everybody, can I talk to Grif alone?"

All but Moss look baffled. They file out, though, leaving me to say, "Everybody's making me to be something special, when none of this would have happened if I hadn't insisted on Dad coming to see me. He wouldn't have taken someone else's flight, or got caught in a storm, or had to fly into an unlighted airport."

"You couldn't help a lightning strike taking out the power, Beatty."

I wish I could leave it at that.

144

"Grif, the landing lights stopped working *before* the airport lost power, maybe when the wind blew over the workbench. If they'd stayed on a just a little longer, then maybe Dad would have seen them and come down safely on his own. So I guess... I mean, if that electrician *could* have arranged time to fix them the other day, if I'd gotten his message to you the way I should have..."

I can tell from Grif's face that his thoughts are following the same path mine are: Whatever blame belongs to me is also his, because I'm his responsibility. And his boss told him, one more slip...

The door opens just then, and Mr. Granger comes in, followed by Moss and Kenzie. He says, "Grif, I've been hearing a story about lost messages and such—all nonsense. None of this would have happened if I hadn't dragged my heels about getting the lights repaired back when you told me it needed doing.

"And I don't want you saying anything different that might lose me the best station manager the Muddy Springs Airport's ever had." He looks my way. "Or one of the best free assistants."

I could hug him, and Grif says, "Mr. Granger... Thank you."

Looking embarrassed, Mr. Granger answers, "It's nothing, compared with all you've done." Then he smiles, no end pleased with himself: "Just air over a plane's wings."

Clo and Annie come back in the room in time to hear this last and join in the laughter.

Kenzie says, "I hope you all ain't thinking that the mess out at the airport is nothing, because cleaning it up is going to be a job." He turns to Moss, "We've got to get that workbench upright, and let's hope nothing important's broke.

"And, Beatty," he says, "you get out on that airfield with a trash bag first thing tomorrow morning. I don't want to find so much as a half-burnt rag left blowing around—"

"Later, Kenzie," Annie interrupts.

"Later what?"

"Beatty can help you later in the day if she wants. But in the morning—she and I have a date."

I see Annie throw a questioning look to Dad, who nods.

"Beatty," Annie asks, "how about a flying lesson?"

Epilogue

S o t h i s i s my dad's world. And my mother's.

And Annie's and Kenzie's, too, even now.

I look behind me as Annie moves controls duplicated by the ones in the student seat where I am. How will she fit into my life after this morning?

Like Moss says, *Who knows?*

But me, I know at this moment who I am and where I belong.

I can almost believe the climbing plane itself is telling me, carrying the message in the low vibration of the ledge where my arm rests, in the force that presses me against my seat.

Below, long sweeps of land drop away as we fly over the Muddy Springs Airport, past Moss's bluff, across mesquite-dotted ground threaded by thicket-lined creekbeds.

We bank in a long, gentle circle, swinging wide around Airfield Road, passing the airport again, not straightening out until we reach the highway. When we're over Joe's Texas Auto Parts, I point down and Annie tips a wing.

A moment later, way below, Joe waves flashing metal to let us know he's seen.

We're flying due east now, and the morning light shines full in my eyes, and for a moment I can feel how it might pull a person into danger.

But I've had a lot more people teaching me than my mother had. And I suppose that is what the hangar flying is, also: flyers passing on what they've learned.

I'll try my best to mind what they've said.

Just let me live part of my life up here, and I'll be respectful. I won't ever fly too close to the sun.

Of course, not *too* close is all I'm promising. That still leaves high, high up, as close as I can safely get....

"Take the stick?" Annie shouts through a speaking tube.

For the first time, I pull back a control column and move it left and press down on a left rudder pedal. The nose of the *Gold Lightning* plane lifts, and one wing dips, and we begin a slow turn to the north.

"Now level out, Beatty," Annie shouts. "Just let up easy."

Level out. Let up. Me, Beatrice Anne Donnough, I'm flying. I am FLYING!

WITHDRAWN

DATE DUE